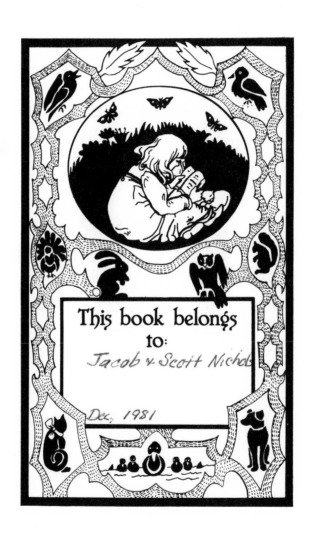

This book belongs
to:
Jacob & Scott Nichols

Dec, 1981

The Platt & Munk
Treasury of
STORIES for CHILDREN

Edited by Nancy Christensen Hall

Cover illustration by Tasha Tudor
Title page illustration by George and Doris Hauman
Designed by Sallie Baldwin

Platt & Munk, Publishers/New York
A Division of Grosset & Dunlap

For Amy and Kirsten—
the Country Mouse and the City Mouse

ACKNOWLEDGMENTS

Grateful acknowledgment is made to the following publishers, authors, artists, and other copyright holders for permission to reprint copyrighted materials:

"The Little Engine That Could" from THE LITTLE ENGINE THAT COULD.™Retold by Watty Piper. Illustrated by George and Doris Hauman. Copyright MCMLXI, MCMLIV, The Platt & Munk Co., Inc. All rights reserved. Also copyright MCMXXX and MCMXLV by The Platt & Munk Co., Inc. From THE PONY ENGINE by Mabel C. Bragg. Copyrighted by George C. Doran & Co. Reprinted by permission of the publisher.

"The Old Time Story of the Three Bears" from THE OLD TIME STORY OF THE THREE BEARS. Originally published by Henry Altemus & Co. Illustrator unknown.

"Teeny-Tiny," "The Boy and the North Wind" and "The Ugly Duckling" from TALES FROM STORYLAND. Edited by Watty Piper. Illustrated by George and Doris Hauman. Copyright MCMXXXVIII and MCMXLI by The Platt & Munk Co., Inc.

"The Country Mouse and the City Mouse," "The Shoemaker and the Elves" and "The Little Turtle That Could Not Stop Talking" from FOLK TALES CHILDREN LOVE. Edited by Watty Piper. Illustrated by Lucille W. and H.C. Holling. Copyright MCMXXXII, MCMXXXIV and MCMLV by The Platt & Munk Co., Inc.

"Little Brown Bear is Afraid of the Dark" from LITTLE BROWN BEAR by Elizabeth Upham. Illustrated by Marjorie Hartwell. Copyright MCMXLII by The Platt & Munk Co., Inc.

"Uncle Wiggily and the Red Spots" from UNCLE WIGGILY AND HIS FRIENDS by Howard R. Garis. Illustrated by George Carlson. Copyright MCMLV, MCMXXXIX, The Platt & Munk Co., Inc. Reprinted by permission of Mabel Garis.

"Little Red Riding Hood" and "Snow-white and Rose-red" from LITTLE RED RIDING HOOD AND OTHER STORIES. Illustrator unknown. Originally published by Hurst & Co.

"The Owl and the Pussy-Cat" by Edward Lear from FIRST POEMS OF CHILDHOOD. Illustrated by Tasha Tudor. Copyright 1967 by Platt & Munk.

"The Fir Tree" from LITTLE RED RIDING HOOD AND OTHER STORIES. Originally published by Hurst & Co. New illustrations done by Anthony Rao.

"A Home for Tandy" from A HOME FOR TANDY by Audrey and Harvey Hirsch. Illustrated by Tim and Greg Hildebrandt. Copyright 1971 by Audrey and Harvey Hirsch. Reprinted by permission of the authors.

"Sleeping Beauty" and "The Goosegirl" from FAMOUS FAIRY TALES. Edited by Watty Piper. Illustrated by Eulalie Banks. Copyright 1922, 1928 and 1933 by The Platt & Munk Co., Inc.

"The Three Billy Goats Gruff" and "The Frog Prince" from TASHA TUDOR'S BEDTIME BOOK. Edited by Kate Klimo. Illustrated by Tasha Tudor. Copyright 1977 by Platt & Munk, Publishers.

"Little Black Sambo" from LITTLE BLACK SAMBO by Helen Bannerman. Illustrated by Eulalie Banks. Copyright 1925, 1928, 1955 and 1972 by Platt & Munk, Publishers.

"Chicken Little" from THE STORY OF CHICKEN LITTLE as retold by Watty Piper. With illustrations from original drawings by Margaret Campbell Hoopes. Copyright MCMXXXV by The Platt & Munk Co., Inc.

"Puss-in-Boots" from PUSS-IN-BOOTS by Reginald Wright Kauffman. Illustrator unknown. Copyright 1922 by Howard E. Altemus.

"Cinderella" from FAMOUS FAIRY TALES. Edited by Watty Piper. Illustrated by Lois Lenski. Copyright 1922, 1928 and 1933 by The Platt & Munk Co., Inc.

CONTENTS

THE LITTLE
ENGINE THAT COULD™

As retold by Watty Piper

Illustrated by George and Doris Hauman

The Little Engine That Could™ is the trademark of Platt & Munk Books.

CHUG, chug, chug. Puff, puff, puff. Ding-dong, ding-dong. The little train rumbled over the tracks. She was a happy little train for she had such a jolly load to carry. Her cars were filled full of good things for boys and girls.

1

There were toy animals—giraffes with long necks, Teddy bears with almost no necks at all, and even a baby elephant. Then there were dolls—dolls with blue eyes and yellow curls, dolls with brown eyes and brown bobbed heads, and the funniest little toy clown you ever saw. And there were cars full of toy engines, airplanes, tops, jack-knives, picture puzzles, books, and every kind of thing boys or girls could want.

But that was not all. Some of the cars were filled with all sorts of good things for

2

boys and girls to eat—big golden oranges, red-cheeked apples, bottles of creamy milk for their breakfasts, fresh spinach for their dinners, peppermint drops and lollypops for after-meal treats.

The little train was carrying all these wonderful things to the good boys and girls on the other side of the mountain. She puffed along merrily. Then all of a sudden she stopped with a jerk. She simply could not go another inch. She tried and she tried, but her wheels would not turn.

What were all those good little boys and girls on the other side of the mountain going to do without the wonderful toys to play with and the good food to eat?

"Here comes a shiny new engine," said the funny little clown who jumped out of the train. "Let us ask him to help us."

So all the dolls and toys cried out together:

"Please, Shiny New Engine, won't you please pull our train over the mountain? Our engine has broken down, and the boys and girls on the other side won't have any toys to play with or good food to eat unless you help us."

But the Shiny New Engine snorted: "I pull you? I am a Passenger Engine. I have just carried a fine big train over the mountain, with more cars than you ever dreamed of. My train had sleeping cars, with comfortable berths; a dining-car where waiters bring whatever hungry people want to eat; and parlor cars in which people sit in soft arm-chairs and look out of big plate-glass windows. I pull the likes of you? Indeed not!" And off he steamed to the round-house, where engines live when they are not busy.

How sad the little train and all the dolls and toys felt! Then the little clown called out, "The Passenger Engine is not the only one in the world. Here is another engine coming, a great big strong one. Let us ask him to help us."

The little toy clown waved his flag and the big strong engine came to a stop.

"Please, oh, please, Big Engine," cried all the dolls and toys together. "Won't you please pull our train over the mountain? Our engine has broken down, and the good little boys and girls on the other side won't have any toys to play with or good food to eat unless you help us."

But the Big Strong Engine bellowed: "I am a Freight Engine. I have just pulled a big train loaded with big machines over the mountain. These machines print books and newspapers for grown-ups to read. I am a very important engine indeed. I won't pull the likes of you!" And the Freight Engine puffed off indignantly to the roundhouse.

The little train and all the dolls and toys were very sad.

"Cheer up," cried the little toy clown. "The Freight Engine is not the only one in the world. Here comes another. He looks old and tired, but our train is so little, perhaps he can help us."

So the little toy clown waved his flag and the dingy, rusty old engine stopped.

"Please, Kind Engine," cried all the dolls and toys together. "Won't you please pull our

6

train over the mountain? Our engine has broken down, and the boys and girls on the other side won't have any toys to play with or good food to eat unless you help us."

But the Rusty Old Engine sighed: "I am so tired. I must rest my weary wheels. I cannot pull even so little a train as yours over the mountain. I can not. I can not. I can not."

And off he rumbled to the roundhouse chugging, "I can not. I can not. I can not."

Then indeed the little train was very, very sad, and the dolls and toys were ready to cry.

But the little clown called out, "Here is another engine coming, a little blue engine, a very little one, maybe she will help us."

The very little engine came chug, chugging merrily along. When she saw the toy clown's flag, she stopped quickly.

"What is the matter, my friends?" she asked kindly.

"Oh, Little Blue Engine," cried the dolls and toys. "Will you pull us over the mountain? Our engine has broken down and the good boys and girls on the other side won't have any toys to play with or good food to eat, unless you help us. Please, please, help us, Little Blue Engine."

"I'm not very big," said the Little Blue Engine. "They use me only for switching trains in the yard. I have never been over the mountain."

"But we must get over the mountain before the children awake," said all the dolls and the toys.

The very little engine looked up and saw the tears in the dolls' eyes. And she thought of the good little boys and girls on the other side of the mountain who would not have any toys or good food unless she helped.

Then she said, "I think I can. I think I can. I think I can." And she hitched herself to the little train.

She tugged and pulled and pulled and tugged and slowly, slowly, slowly they started off.

The toy clown jumped aboard and all the dolls and the toy animals began to smile and cheer.

Puff, puff, chug, chug, went the Little Blue Engine. "I think I can—I think I can—I think I can—I think I can—I think I can—I think I can—I think I can—I think I can—I think I can."

Up, up, up. Faster and faster and faster and faster the little engine climbed, until at last they reached the top of the mountain.

Down in the valley lay the city.

"Hurray, hurray," cried the funny little clown and all the dolls and toys. "The good little boys and girls in the city will be happy because you helped us, kind Little Blue Engine."

And the Little Blue Engine smiled and seemed to say as she puffed steadily down the mountain:

"I thought I could. I thought I could. I thought I could.

I thought I could.

I thought I could.

I thought I could."

THE OLD TIME STORY OF THE THREE BEARS

ONCE upon a time there were Three Bears who lived in a cozy little cottage built just for three. In another house, at the other end of the woods, lived a pretty little girl who took long walks through the woods and often strayed far from home. Her hair was so golden that everyone called her Goldilocks.

One day Goldilocks came to the house in the woods where the Three Bears lived. She looked in the window, and seeing nobody in the house, she turned the handle of the door.

The door was not fastened, so Goldilocks went right in. There on the table she found three bowls of porridge.

If she had been a thoughtful little girl, she would have waited till the bears came home, and then, perhaps, they would have invited her to join them for breakfast.

But the porridge looked tempting, so she helped herself. First she tasted the porridge of the Great Big Bear, but that was too hot. Next she tasted the porridge of the Middle Sized Bear, but that was too cold. Then she tasted the porridge of the Little Small Wee Bear, and that was neither too hot nor too cold, but just right. So she ate it all up.

Then Goldilocks saw three chairs by the wall. First she sat in the chair of the Great Big Bear, but that was too hard. Next she sat in the chair of the Middle Sized Bear, but that was too soft. Then she sat in the chair of the Little Small Wee Bear, and that was neither too hard nor too soft, but just right, until the bottom of the chair fell out.

Then Goldilocks went into the bedroom where the Three Bears slept. First she lay down upon the bed of the Great Big Bear, but that was too high at the head. Next she lay down upon the bed of the Middle Sized

10

Bear, and that was too high at the foot. Then she lay down upon the bed of the Little Small Wee Bear, and that was just right. So she covered herself up and fell fast asleep.

By this time the Three Bears returned home for breakfast.

First the Great Big Bear noticed that the spoon had been taken out of his bowl. "SOMEBODY HAS BEEN TASTING MY PORRIDGE!" he said in his great, gruff voice.

And the Middle Sized Bear noticed that her spoon was in her bowl. "SOMEBODY HAS BEEN TASTING MY PORRIDGE!" she said in her middle sized voice.

Then the Little Small Wee Bear looked at his bowl, but the porridge was all gone. "Somebody has been tasting *my* porridge and has eaten it all up!" he cried in his little small wee voice.

Next the same thing happened with the chairs.

And you know what Goldilocks had done to the third chair.

Then the Three Bears began to look around and went into their bedroom. First the Great Big Bear noticed that his pillow was out of place. "SOMEBODY HAS BEEN LYING IN MY BED!" he said, in his great, gruff voice.

Then the Middle Sized Bear noticed that the coverlet was out of place on her bed. "SOMEBODY HAS BEEN LYING ON MY BED!" she said in her middle sized voice.

And when the Little Small Wee Bear looked at his bed, there was Goldilocks—fast asleep. "Somebody has been lying in *my* bed, and here she is!" said the little small wee voice.

When Goldilocks heard the little small wee voice of the Little Small Wee Bear, it was so sharp and so shrill that it awakened her at once.

Up she started; and when she saw the Three Bears at the side of the bed, she tumbled out at the other side and ran to the window.

Luckily, the window was open, and she jumped right out and ran away as fast as she could. What happened to her afterwards, I cannot tell. But the Three Bears never saw her again.

TEENY-TINY

Illustrated by George and Doris Hauman

ONCE upon a time there was a teeny-tiny woman. Everything about her was teeny-tiny. She lived in a teeny-tiny cottage in a teeny-tiny village. She had a teeny-tiny cat that caught teeny-tiny mice in a teeny-tiny cellar.

One fine day this teeny-tiny woman put on her teeny-tiny bonnet and said to her teeny-tiny cat:

"I think I'll take a teeny-tiny walk this lovely day."

"Meow," replied the teeny-tiny cat. "Go if you like. I'd rather stay in this teeny-tiny house by the teeny-tiny fireplace and catch some teeny-tiny mice."

So the teeny-tiny woman went out of her teeny-tiny cottage and started along the teeny-tiny street in the teeny-tiny village. Pretty soon she came to a teeny-tiny gate in a teeny-tiny fence that enclosed a teeny-tiny garden. In the middle of the teeny-tiny garden the teeny-tiny woman saw a teeny-tiny scarecrow. It was wearing a teeny-tiny dress and a teeny-tiny bonnet.

"That teeny-tiny scarecrow has better clothes than I have," said the teeny-tiny woman to herself. "I think I'll take them back to my teeny-tiny cottage."

So she opened the teeny-tiny gate and walked up to the teeny-tiny scarecrow.

"Don't take clothes that belong to someone else," whispered the teeny-tiny woman's teeny-tiny conscience in a teeny-tiny voice.

"It isn't *someone*," said the teeny-tiny woman. "It's only a teeny-tiny scarecrow." So she took the teeny-tiny dress and the teeny-tiny bonnet from the teeny-tiny scarecrow and carried them to her teeny-tiny cottage.

When she got there, the teeny-tiny woman took off her teeny-tiny clothes and put on the teeny-tiny dress she had taken from the teeny-tiny scarecrow. She hung her own teeny-tiny dress and bonnet and the teeny-tiny scarecrow's teeny-tiny bonnet in the teeny-tiny clothes closet in her teeny-tiny bedroom.

Just as she was going down the teeny-tiny stairs from her teeny-tiny bedroom, her teeny-tiny cat came up the teeny-tiny stairs from the teeny-tiny cellar.

"Meow," said the teeny-tiny cat. "That isn't your teeny-tiny dress."

"Oh, yes it is," said the teeny-tiny woman, and she went about her teeny-tiny work.

That night when she went up the teeny-tiny stairs to her teeny-tiny bedroom, she took off the teeny-tiny dress she had taken from the teeny-tiny scarecrow and hung it in the teeny-tiny closet. Soon she was fast asleep in her teeny-tiny bed.

But it wasn't very long before she was wakened by a teeny-tiny voice, which came from the teeny-tiny closet.

"Give me my clothes!"

said the teeny-tiny voice. At this the teeny-tiny woman was a teeny-tiny bit frightened. She called out in her teeny-tiny voice:

"Who's there?"

When there was no reply, she pulled the teeny-tiny bedclothes up over her teeny-tiny head and went to sleep again.

But in a little while she was wakened by the same voice, and this time it was a teeny-tiny bit louder.

"GIVE ME MY CLOTHES!"

it said. The teeny-tiny woman was a teeny-tiny bit more frightened. But she didn't answer. She just hid her teeny-tiny head under the teeny-tiny bedclothes again and went back to sleep.

Pretty soon she was wakened for the third time. And now the teeny-tiny voice wasn't teeny-tiny at all. It was very loud and angry.

"GIVE ME MY CLOTHES!"

it shouted. The teeny-tiny woman put her teeny-tiny head out of her teeny-tiny bedclothes and shouted back, as loud as she could, with her teeny-tiny voice:

"TAKE 'EM!"

THE COUNTRY MOUSE AND THE CITY MOUSE

Illustrated by Lucille W. and H. C. Holling

A LITTLE mouse who lived in the country once invited his city cousin to come and visit him. When the country mouse had shown the city mouse the green fields and the big red barn, they sat down to a dinner of barley and grain.

The country mouse was hungry and ate heartily, but the city mouse only nibbled daintily.

"Don't you like this barley and grain?" asked the country mouse.

"Not very well, dear Cousin," answered the city mouse. "I don't want to seem impolite, but I wish you could come to the city and visit me. I will show you what good food is."

"I should like to come very much, dear Cousin," said the country mouse.

One day not long afterwards, the country mouse came to the city to visit his cousin in his grand townhouse.

"You must be hungry after your trip from the country," said the city mouse. "We will go to the pantry and you shall have a feast," and he led the way through a hole into the kitchen pantry.

The country mouse had never seen so many jars and bags and boxes in all his life as there were on the shelves. His mouth began to water as they scampered along the lowest shelf.

"Oh, what luck!" cried the city mouse. "Someone has left the cake box open."

They crept inside and the country mouse saw something big and round and brown.

"This chocolate cake is a little dry," said the city mouse, "but see how you like it."

The little country mouse nibbled at the big, round, brown thing. How sweet it was! He had never tasted anything more delicious. What a wonderful house his cousin had!

The two little mice nibbled away happily.

"How very lucky you are, dear Cousin," the country mouse started to say, when the door opened. A big, rosy-cheeked woman with a mixing-bowl in her hands came into the pantry.

"Shhhh," whispered the city mouse, "run quickly for the hole."

The two little mice scampered along the shelf and back into the hole. When they were safe inside, the city mouse said, "Don't look frightened, Cousin. That was only the cook. She was going to make a fresh cake and wanted some sugar and flour. She hates mice, but she's too slow to catch us. She will not stay long in the pantry. We will go back in a few minutes for I have many other things to show you."

After a little while, the city mouse looked out of the hole and saw that the cook had gone.

"Come on," he called to his cousin, and back they scampered to the pantry shelf.

This time the city mouse showed his country cousin a box. "There is something good inside," he said, and they began to gnaw a hole in one corner as fast as they could.

When they had gnawed through the cardboard, the country mouse tasted something he thought was even more delicious than the chocolate cake. The city mouse told him that the box was filled with raisins.

"What fun it is to have such fine things to eat every day," the country mouse was thinking, when he heard a scratching at the door and a queer meowing sound.

"Run, run," whispered the city mouse.

When they were safely back in the hole again, the city mouse said, "Don't tremble so,

dear Cousin, that was only the cat. Of course she likes to eat mice and she is very good at catching us in her sharp claws, but she will soon go away."

The country mouse was so frightened he could not stop trembling.

"I would rather not go back to the pantry, dear Cousin, if you don't mind," he said.

"All right," said the city mouse. "The very best foods for mice are in the cellar cupboard. The cat is in the kitchen, so we are safe."

They scampered down the stairs into the cellar cupboard. The country mouse gazed round in astonishment. It was the most wonderful place he had ever seen. There were ever so many more things there than in the kitchen pantry.

On the floor were barrels of delicious-smelling apples. From the ceiling hung strings of sausages. On the shelves there were jars and bottles and boxes and bags. Some of the jars were filled with golden butter, and some with red jelly and jam. In the bags were all sorts of good-smelling things.

The two little mice scampered about, nibbling here and there at anything they could find open.

Then the country mouse saw something that was a deep yellow color. It smelled very good. He took a nibble. It had a most delicious taste.

"That is cheese," his city cousin told him. "There is really nothing better than cheese."

The country mouse saw another piece of cheese that looked and smelled even better than the piece he had just nibbled. It was fastened to a queer little round stand. He was just about to take a big bite of this piece of cheese when the city mouse called out:

"Stop, stop, don't eat that cheese. It is in a trap."

"What is a trap?" asked the country mouse. "I never heard of one."

"If you touch the cheese in a trap," said the city mouse, "something hard comes down on your neck. You cannot breathe any more. You can never nibble cake or cheese again."

"Oh," said the country mouse, trembling from his whiskers to his tail. "I think I must be going home right away. You have been very kind to give me all these fine things to eat, dear Cousin. The cake and the raisins and the cheese were delicious, but I would rather eat my barley and grain and be safe than to feast like a king and live in terror."

So the little country mouse went home to the country and ate barley and grain in peace and comfort for the rest of his days.

LITTLE BROWN BEAR
IS AFRAID OF THE DARK

By Elizabeth Upham
Illustrated by Marjorie Hartwell

IT was Little Brown Bear's bedtime.
"Good night, Mother Bear. Good night, Father Bear," he said.
"Good night, Little Brown Bear," said Mother Bear and Father Bear.
Then Little Brown Bear picked up his red candle and went upstairs, singing:

> "Riddledly-red, Riddledy-red!
> Up the stairs and away to bed!"

Little Brown Bear put the candle on the table. Then he took off his new blue suit and hung it in the closet. After that he put his best brown shoes under the chair. Then he put on the striped pajamas that Grandma Bear had given him. And the next moment—pop! he was in bed, leaving the candle for Mother Bear to blow out.

> "I let my candle burn at night,
> For I'm afraid without a light,"

he said to himself.
Yellow Moon looked in through the open window.

> "Ha, ha, ha! Ho, ho, ho!
> That's the funniest thing I know,"

laughed Yellow Moon.

"What is funny?" asked Little Brown Bear.

"Being afraid of the dark," said Yellow Moon.

"Isn't everyone afraid of the dark?" asked Little Brown Bear, very much surprised.

"Oh, no, indeed!" said Yellow Moon. "Come over to the window, and you'll soon find out."

So Little Brown Bear jumped out of bed and went over to the window.

A black cricket was chirping cheerily nearby.

"You're afraid of the dark, aren't you, Black Cricket?" Little Brown Bear called out to him.

"My goodness, no! indeed I'm not.
I really like the dark a lot!"

chirped Black Cricket.

Wise Old Owl was hooting from the butternut tree nearby.

"You're afraid of the dark, aren't you, Wise Old Owl?" Little Brown Bear called out to him.

"To whit, to whoo! to whit, to whee!
The darkness is my time to see,"

hooted Wise Old Owl.

Green Frog was croaking in the pond not far away.

"Aren't you afraid of the dark, Green Frog?" asked Little Brown Bear.

"The dark is fine, it seems to me.
I'm not afraid, oh, no, siree!"

croaked Green Frog.

Just then Mr. Wind came right into the room.

"I think it must be a lot of fun to lie in bed and listen to Wise Old Owl and Black Cricket and Green Frog, and to watch Yellow Moon shining in through the window," he said. "Wouldn't you like to try it, Little Brown Bear?"

"It might be fun. I do not know.
But I can try if you say so,"

said Little Brown Bear.

"Then hop into bed and close your eyes," said Mr. Wind.

At that Little Brown Bear hopped into bed and closed his eyes.

"Pouf! Pouf!" blew Mr. Wind.

And out went Little Brown Bear's candle.

"Now open your eyes, and you will see
What a very nice thing the dark can be,"

said Mr. Wind.

So Little Brown Bear opened his eyes. He saw Yellow Moon shining in at him, and he heard Black Cricket chirping outside his window and Wise Old Owl hooting in the butternut tree and Green Frog croaking in the pond.

"A bed in the dark is lots of fun!
It shouldn't frighten anyone!"

sang Little Brown Bear.

And in no time at all he was fast asleep.

UNCLE WIGGILY
AND THE RED SPOTS

By Howard R. Garis

Illustrated by George Carlson

See the red and horrid spots!
Yes, there are just lots and lots.
Nurse is making quite a fuss,

Doctor looks so serious.
Here's the answer, if we look
At the story in the book.

UNCLE Wiggily Longears was hopping along through the woods one fine day, when he heard a little voice calling to him:

"Oh, Uncle Wiggily! Will you have a game of tag with me?"

At first the bunny uncle thought the voice might belong to a bad fox or harum-scarum bear, but when he had peeked through the bushes he saw that it was Lulu Wibblewobble, the duck girl.

"Have a game of tag with you? Why, of course I will!" laughed Uncle Wiggily. "That is, if you will kindly excuse my rheumatism, and my red, white and blue crutch."

"Of course I'll excuse it, Uncle Wiggily," said Lulu. "Only please don't tag me with the end of your crutch, for it tickles me, and when I'm tickled I have to laugh, and when I laugh I can't play tag."

"I won't," said Uncle Wiggily with a laugh.

So the little duck girl and the rabbit gentleman played tag in the woods.

Sometimes Lulu was "it" and Uncle Wiggily would be tagged by the foot or the wing of the duck girl.

"Now for a last tag!" cried Uncle Wiggily when it was getting late. "I'll tag you this time, Lulu, and then we must go home." And they ran right into a berry bush.

"I guess I can't tag you this time, Lulu," laughed the bunny uncle. "We'll give up the game now, and I'll be 'it' next time we play."

"All right, Uncle Wiggily," said Lulu. "I'll meet you here in the woods at this time tomorrow and I'll bring Alice and Jimmie with me, and we'll play tag again and have lots of fun."

"Fine!" said the bunny uncle, as he squirmed his way out of the bush.

Then he went on to his hollow stump bungalow, and Lulu went on to her duck pen house to have her supper of corn and meal.

As Uncle Wiggily was sitting down to his supper of carrot ice cream with lettuce sandwiches, Nurse Jane Fuzzy Wuzzy looked at him and exclaimed:

"Why, Wiggily! What's the matter with you?"

"Matter with me? Nothing. I feel just fine!" he said.

"Why, you're all covered with red spots!" went on the muskrat lady, "you are breaking out with the measles. I must send for Dr. Possum at once."

"Measles? Nonsense!" exclaimed Uncle Wiggily. "I can't have measles again. I've had them once."

"Well, you are certainly all covered with red spots, and red spots are always measles," said the muskrat lady.

"You must go to bed at once," said Nurse Jane, "and when Dr. Possum comes he'll tell you what else to do."

Uncle Wiggily looked at himself in a glass to make sure.

"Well, I guess I have the measles all right," he said. "But I don't see how I can have them twice. This must be a different kind than I had before."

It was dark when Dr. Possum came, and when he saw the red spots on Uncle Wiggily, he said:

"Yes, I guess they are measles all right. Lots of the animal children are down with them. But don't worry. Keep warm and quiet, and you'll be all right in a few days."

So Uncle Wiggily went to bed, red spots and all. Nurse Jane made him hot carrot and sassafras tea with whipped cream and chocolate in it.

All the next day the bunny uncle stayed in bed with his red spots. He wanted very much to go out in the woods looking for an adventure.

When evening came and Nurse Jane was sitting out on the front porch of the hollow stump bungalow, she suddenly heard a quacking sound.

Coming up the path were Lulu, Alice and Jimmie Wibblewobble, the duck children.

29

"Where is Uncle Wiggily?" asked Lulu.

"He is in bed," answered Nurse Jane.

"Why is he in bed?" asked Jimmie. "Was he bad?"

"No, indeed," laughed Nurse Jane. "But your Uncle Wiggily is in bed because he has the red-spotted measles. What did you want of him?"

"He promised to meet us in the woods," answered Lulu, "and play tag with us. We waited and waited and played tag all by ourselves, even jumping in the bush, as Uncle Wiggily accidentally did when he was chasing me yesterday. So we came here to see what is the matter."

As the three duck children came up on the porch, where the bright light shone on them, Nurse Jane said:

"Oh, my goodness me! You ducks are all covered with red spots, too! You all have the measles! Oh, my!"

"Measles!" cried Jimmie, the boy duck. "Measles? These aren't measles, Nurse Jane! They are sticky, red berries from the bushes we jumped in as Uncle Wiggily did. The red berries are sticky, like burdock burrs, and they stuck to us."

"Oh, my goodness!" cried Nurse Jane. "Wait a minute, children!" Then she ran to where Uncle Wiggily was lying in bed. She leaned over and picked off some of the red spots from his fur.

"Why!" cried the muskrat lady. "You haven't the measles at all, Wiggily! It's just sticky, red berries in your fur, just as they are in the ducks' feathers. You're all right. Get up and have a good time!"

And Uncle Wiggily did and Nurse Jane combed the red, sticky burr-berries out of his fur. He didn't have the measles at all, for which he was very glad.

"My goodness! That certainly was a funny mistake for all of us," said Dr. Possum next day. "But the red spots surely did look like the measles." Which shows us that things are not always what they seem.

31

THE BOY AND THE NORTH WIND

Illustrated by George and Doris Hauman

LONG ago, in Norway, a boy lived with his mother. One day she gave him a bowl and said, "Go to the storehouse and bring me some meal for our porridge."

The boy crossed the yard and filled the bowl in the storehouse. But the moment he came out of the doorway, the North Wind came up with a roar and blew all the meal from the bowl.

So the boy went back into the storehouse and got some more meal, but as soon as he stepped out of the door, the Wind blew the meal away again. Once more he filled the bowl, and once more the Wind emptied it.

Then the boy was angry. He started walking toward the North, where the Wind had his home. He walked and walked, and it was almost night when he reached the palace of the North Wind.

"Good day," said the boy to the Wind. "Thank you for calling on me yesterday."

"Good day," the Wind replied gruffly. "There's no need of thanks. What has brought you here?"

"I came to ask you to give back the meal you blew from my bowl," said the boy. "We are very poor, and if you keep blowing our meal away, we are likely to starve."

32

"I have no meal," said the North Wind, "but I'll give you a tablecloth that will be better than many bushels of grain. When you want to eat, say to the cloth, 'Cloth, cover the table and serve a fine meal.' "

The boy thanked the North Wind and started home with the tablecloth, but darkness came upon him before he had gone far. There was an inn nearby and the boy stepped inside. He seated himself and said, "Cloth, cover the table and serve a fine meal." Immediately a delicious dinner was before him.

The other guests in the inn were wonderstruck, and the innkeeper's wife immediately determined that the tablecloth should belong to her. In the middle of the night she crept to the room where the boy was asleep and took the cloth from him. In its place she left one of her own that looked very much like it.

When he reached home, the boy told his mother all his adventures and showed her the tablecloth. "It is a magic cloth," he said, "and serves a meal whenever I tell it to."

"I'll believe it when I see it," said his mother.

The boy put the cloth on the table and said, "Cloth, cover the table and serve a fine meal." But the cloth lay just as he had put it without stirring an inch, for of course it was not the magic cloth.

"Well," said the boy, "I'll have to go back to the North Wind and tell him his table-cloth is no good." And when he trudged into the palace of the North Wind he was feeling very angry.

"That tablecloth that you gave me is no good," he declared. "It worked once in the inn, but when I reached home it had lost its magic."

"Someone must have robbed you," replied the North Wind. "I have no more table-cloths, but here is a goat that will keep you supplied with money. When your purse is empty, say, 'Goat, give me gold,' and immediately it will be filled with gold coins."

The boy thanked the Wind and led the goat to the same inn where he had spent the previous night. He knew that his purse was empty, so he said, "Goat, give me gold." Immediately, to the astonishment and envy of the innkeeper, the purse was full of golden coins.

That night the innkeeper crept to the place where the boy was sleeping and led the goat away. In its place he left one of his own goats.

When the boy reached home, he told his mother about the goat's power to fill his purse with gold.

"I'll believe it when I see it," said his mother.

The boy gave the order, "Goat, give me gold," but of course no gold appeared. The boy was angrier than ever. Back he went to the palace of the North Wind and told him the goat would not give gold.

"Well," said the North Wind, "I have nothing left to give you except that old stick you see standing in the corner. If you say to it, 'Stick, lay on,' it will beat anyone who is bothering you. When you want it to stop, say, 'Stick, leave off.' "

This time when he came to the inn, the boy resolved that he would not fall asleep. He lay down and pretended to be asleep, but he kept himself awake. At length he heard the innkeeper creeping toward him. The innkeeper had not seen the stick do anything, but he felt sure it must have some such magic, as the tablecloth and the goat had. So he resolved to steal it.

Just as he was reaching for it, the boy opened his eyes and said, "Stick, lay on."

Up jumped the stick and began to beat the innkeeper. He ran around the room, jumping over tables and chairs, but could not get away from the stick.

"Please, please save me." he cried. "Call to your stick to stop and I'll give back the tablecloth and the goat."

The boy gave the order. "Stick, leave off," and immediately it jumped into his hand and was still.

Then the innkeeper brought out the tablecloth and the goat, and the boy started for home happily, swinging the stick in his hand. When he reached the cottage, he said, "Cloth, cover the table and serve a fine meal." And there before his mother's eyes was the finest dinner she had ever seen. Then he said, "Goat, give me gold," and his purse was piled with golden coins. "We shall never have to worry about a bowlful of meal again," said the boy, "and we'll keep the stick standing in the corner, to be used if anyone tries to rob us of our tablecloth or our goat." And they lived forever after in peace and prosperity.

LITTLE RED RIDING HOOD

ONCE upon a time, in an ancient forest of Brittany, there dwelt a woodman and his wife, who had only one child—a little daughter. She was so beautiful, so good, so tender, and so kind, that everybody loved her. Her grandmother, who dwelt in the midst of the wood, made her a little red cloak and hood, which became her glossy black hair and sparkling hazel eyes so well that people called her Little Red Riding Hood.

She dwelt in a pleasant home, green glades stretched all around it, beautiful wild flowers grew under the trees—silvery may bluebells, wild thyme, oxlips, cowslips, and primroses all in their season; and in the ripe autumn, there were hazel-nuts and blackberries. And the birds and the squirrels were Red Riding Hood's playfellows, in addition to the great wolfhound, Bran, who loved her dearly and was seldom happy when she was out of his sight.

One fine day, when Red Riding Hood came down to breakfast, she was surprised to see her father all dressed in his best green suit, which he wore only on Sundays.

"Oh, father!" cried she, "where are you going? It is not Sunday."

"No, my child, but there is a great archery show today, and I am going to attend it. I shall take Bran and we'll return this evening."

By and by Red Riding Hood's mother said to her:

"Red Riding Hood, since father is going out, you will not have to carry his dinner into the wood today. I shall send you to your grandmother's instead."

"Oh, mother dear, I shall be so glad to go!" said the little one.

"The dear old lady has been very ill for a long time now," added Red Riding Hood's mother, "and never, I think, gets up; she is quite bed-ridden. Winifred, her little servant, has asked leave for the day, and poor granny is all alone. So I thought that you could go and stay with her a little while and take a basket of nice things to her."

"That I shall gladly," said the little girl.

"Here, my dear," her mother said, "is the basket for your grandmamma, and this little packet on top is for you. You will find in it some bread and butter and cold meat. Get your red cloak and hood, dear, and I shall tie it on."

Little Red Riding Hood obeyed. And her mother tied on her scarlet hood and kissed her good-bye. So Red Riding Hood set off on her errand.

It was still early. The gossamer dew was all over the grass, sparkling in the sunshine like diamonds, and the lark was singing sweetly. And Red Riding Hood peeped about to see if she could find his nest in the grass, but she could not.

By and by she came to a glade full of foxgloves, pink and white; and since she dearly loved flowers, she gathered a great bunch of them.

"They will make grandmamma's chamber look quite gay and remind her of the beautiful summer out of doors," she thought. "Ah, and here are violets down among the moss. I must have some of these."

And she gathered a lovely bouquet, while Ralph, the raven, picked about finding worms, and Lily, the dove, sat on a bough close by and cooed softly to please her.

And then, since she had gathered as many flowers as she liked, Red Riding Hood ran gaily on. She had not advanced ten yards when a large dog, something like Bran, came trotting towards her and said:

"Good-morning, Little Red Riding Hood."

"Good-morning," said the little girl.

The dog—alas! it was really a wolf—turned and trotted along by the side of her, although the raven croaked and gave his heels a sly bite.

"Where are you going, Little Red Riding Hood?" asked the wolf.

"I am going to see grandmamma," replied the child. "She lives at the cottage beneath the elms in the forest."

"Ah, I know her!" said the wolf. "Rather an old lady, is she not?"

"Yes," said Little Red Riding Hood, "and such a dear, kind, gentle granny. I wish she were not so feeble. I am carrying her a basket of nice things to eat as a present."

"Oh?" asked the wolf, putting his nose to the side of the basket. "I suppose she has teeth, then?"

"I don't know," replied Red Riding Hood innocently. "It is so long since I have seen her that I quite forget."

"But how will she let you in? Does she have a nurse?" asked the wolf.

"Her nurse is out, so I shall rap and she will say, 'Pull the string and the latch will come up.' Then I shall do so and go in."

"That is very convenient," said the wolf. And he longed to eat Red Riding Hood up; but woodmen were working nearby, and he could hear their axes. He feared if he flew at Red Riding Hood she would scream, and that they would hurry to her assistance. So he thought of another plan. "Well, Red Riding Hood," he said, "I am obliged to make haste home. Good-morning, I wish you a pleasant walk."

"Good-bye," said Red Riding Hood, and the wolf trotted off very fast.

By now Red Riding Hood was hungry, so she sat down under the trees and opened her packet, took out her bread and cold venison and began to eat her dinner, sharing it, of course, with Ralph and Lily.

By the time Little Red Riding Hood had dined, the sun was high above the trees, and she knew it was getting late, so she rose and set off again.

Meantime, the wicked wolf trotted heavily on till he reached the cottage in the wood. He tapped at the door.

"Who is there?" said a feeble voice inside.

"Little Red Riding Hood," replied the wolf, feigning the child's tones.

"Come in, my love. Pull the string and the latch will come up," said the aged woman from her bed. And the wicked wolf went in.

It was a neat little chamber into which he trotted. There was a great four-post bed with curtains on one side of the room, and in it lay the poor old woman, looking very meek, and patient, and nice.

She was dreadfully frightened, as you may suppose, when she saw the wolf come in instead of her little grandchild. But the savage creature did not give her time to wonder. He made one bound at her and frightened her so that she sprang out of bed on the other side and hid herself in the closet, leaving him entangled in the bed clothes. When the wolf found that he had lost this chance for a dinner, he slipped on the nightcap that grandma had dropped in her haste, and crept into the bed.

Now, while this was going on, Little Red Riding Hood was skipping past the wild rose bushes and through the gate at the end of the wood. She reached her grandmother's cottage just as the wolf had settled himself snugly beneath the clothes.

Little Red Riding Hood knocked at the door.

"Who is there?" said a soft voice.

"Little Red Riding Hood," she replied.

"Come in, my love. Pull the string and the latch will come up."

And Little Red Riding Hood went in.

"Oh! grandmother," she exclaimed, as she reached the bed, "what big ears you have!"

"All the better to hear you with, my dear."

"But what big eyes you have, grandmother!"

"All the better to see you with, my dear."

"But, grandmother, what a big nose you have!"

"All the better to smell you with, my dear."

"And what big teeth you have, grandmother!"

"All the better to eat you with, my dear!" And with these words the wolf sprang at Little Red Riding Hood. Of course he meant to gobble her up.

Little Red Riding Hood screamed for help as loudly as she could.

Just then a woodman, who had been working not far from her grandmother's cottage, heard her cry for help and paused in his work to learn the direction of the sound. When he perceived that the noise came from the cottage he ran quickly there, axe in hand.

So just at the moment that the wolf was about to seize Little Red Riding Hood, he sprang through the door, and with one blow of his axe killed the wolf. Then the child's grandmother came out of the closet and joined them.

"You see, my darling," she said gently, "that one should never loiter on an errand, nor tell one's affairs to strangers, for many a wolf looks like an honest dog."

And when the story was told, everybody was happy that Little Red Riding Hood and her grandmother had escaped the cruel wolf.

THE OWL AND THE PUSSY-CAT

By Edward Lear

Illustrated by Tasha Tudor

The Owl and the Pussy-cat went to sea
    In a beautiful pea-green boat:
They took some honey and plenty of money
    Wrapped up in a five-pound note.
The Owl looked up to the stars above,
    And sang to a small guitar,
"O lovely Pussy, O Pussy, my love,
    What a beautiful Pussy you are,
      You are,
      You are!
What a beautiful Pussy you are!"

Pussy said the Owl, "You elegant fowl,
    How charmingly sweet you sing!
Oh! let us be married; too long we have tarried:
    But what shall we do for a ring?"
They sailed away for a year and a day,
    To the land where the bong-tree grows;
And there in a wood a Piggy-wig stood,
    With a ring at the end of his nose,
        His nose,
        His nose,
    With a ring at the end of his nose.

"Dear Pig, are you willing to sell for one shilling
    Your ring?" Said the Piggy, "I will."
So they took it away, and were married next day
    By the Turkey who lives on the hill.
They dined on mince and slices of quince,
    Which they ate with a runcible spoon;
And hand in hand, on the edge of the sand,
    They danced by the light of the moon,
        The moon,
        The moon,
They danced by the light of the moon.

THE FIR TREE

Illustrated by Anthony Rao

OUT in the forest grew a pretty little Fir Tree. It had a good situation, for it stood well in the sunlight and had sufficient air, while all around were many larger companions, both pines and firs. But the little Fir Tree was so busy with growing that it did not think of the warm sun and the fresh air; nor did it take any notice of the peasant children who roamed about and chattered while they gathered strawberries or raspberries. They would often come with a whole potful, or with the fruit strung upon a straw, and sitting down beside the little Tree would say: "Oh! what a very pretty little Tree this is!" But the Fir Tree was not at all pleased to hear this.

The next year it grew one long joint taller, and the year after it had grown yet another, for on a Fir Tree you can always see by the number of rings how many years it has lived.

"Ah! if only I were as tall a tree as the others," sighed the little Fir; "I could then spread my branches far around and look out from the top of my crown over the wide world. Birds would come and nestle between my boughs, and when the wind blew, I could nod just as proudly as the rest."

It took no pleasure in the sunshine, nor in the birds, nor in the rosy clouds that, morning and evening, went floating past.

In the winter-time, when all around the snow lay dazzlingly white, a hare would now and then come running along and jump right over the little Tree. How ashamed the Fir Tree was! But two winters went by, and when the third year came, the Tree was so big that the hare had to go round it.

"Oh! to grow, to grow, to be large, to be tall, to be old—that is the only desirable thing in the world," thought the Tree.

In the autumn the wood-cutters came and felled some of the tallest trees. This happened every year, and the young Fir, which was now beginning to be grown up, trembled as its huge companions fell with a crash to the ground. The branches were cut away, and they looked quite naked, long and slender—indeed, it was nearly impossible to recognize them. Then they were placed on carts, and horses hauled them away out of the forest. To what place were they going? What was to become of them?

When, in the spring, the Swallow and the Stork came, the Tree said to them: "Do you not know to what place they are taken? Have you not met them?"

The Swallow knew nothing about it; but the Stork looked thoughtful, nodded its head, and said: "Yes, I think I know; I met many ships when I flew away from Egypt, and on the ships were magnificent masts. These, I think, were trees, for they smelt of pine. They were very stately, I can assure you."

"If only I were tall enough to fly away over the sea! What is it—the sea? How does it really look?"

"That would take rather a long time to explain," said the Stork, and he went away.

"Rejoice while you are young," said the Sunbeams. "Rejoice in your fresh growth and in the young life that is in you." And the wind kissed the Fir Tree, the dew shed tears over it; but this the Tree did not understand.

When Christmas-time approached, many young trees were felled, trees that were not even as tall nor as old as our Fir Tree, which never felt any rest, but was always wishing to get away. These young trees —and they were the prettiest of all —were allowed to keep their branches; they were laid on wagons, and the horses hauled them out of the forest. "Where are they going?" asked the Fir Tree. "They are not taller than I—in fact, there was one that was much smaller. Why are they allowed to keep all their branches? To what place are they taken?"

"We know," chirped the Sparrows; "down in the town we have peeped in through the windows, and have seen them planted in the middle of the warm room, dressed in the most beautiful things—gilded apples, gingercakes, toys, and hundreds of candles."

"And then," said the Fir Tree, while every branch trembled, "and then what happens?"

"We have not seen any more, but what we did see was marvelous."

"I wonder whether I have been born to tread this glorious path," cried the Fir Tree, full of joy. "It would be even better than crossing the seas. I am weary with longing. How I wish it were Christmas now; I am quite as tall and well-grown as the others that were taken away last year. Ah! if only I were already on the wagon—if I were in the warm room, surrounded by all that pomp and splendor! And then—yes—something even better will happen—something even more charming—or why should they adorn me so? There must certainly be something even more delightful still—but what is it? Oh! how I long for it! I scarcely know what is the matter with me."

"Rejoice with us," said the Air and the Sunshine; "rejoice in your fresh youth out under

the bright sky." But it would not rejoice, although it grew taller and taller. Winter and summer it stood there in its dark green foliage. Everybody who saw it said: "This is a beautiful tree!" and at Christmas it was felled the first of all. The ax cut deep through the sap, and the Tree fell with a sigh to the earth. It felt a sensation of faintness and could not even think of its happiness. Now it was sad at parting from home—from the spot where it had grown. It knew that it would see the dear old companions no more, nor the little bushes and flowers that grew around; nor, perhaps, the birds. The parting and the journey were, indeed, by no means pleasant.

The Tree did not recover until it was unloaded with the other trees in the yard. It heard a man say: "This is a beautiful tree; we shall only want this one." Then came two servants in full livery and carried the Fir Tree into a large and beautiful hall. Portraits hung upon the walls, and by the huge fireplace stood china vases, silk covered sofas, and large tables covered with picture-books worth a fortune—at least the children said so. The Fir Tree was put into a big tub filled with sand; but nobody could see that it was a tub, for it was draped with foliage and placed on a large carpet of many colors. Oh! how the Tree trembled. What was going to happen? Both the servants and the young ladies began to decorate the Tree. On one branch they hung small nets cut out of colored paper, and each net was filled with sweetmeats; on others were gilded apples and walnuts, looking just as if they had grown there. More than a hundred little candles, red, blue, and white, were fastened to the branches; dolls as real as life—the Tree had never seen such things before—were standing amongst the foliage; and high up at the top shone a great star of tinsel gold—it was splendid; it was simply magnificent!

"This evening," they all said, "this evening it will shine."

"Ah!" thought the Tree, "how I wish it were evening already—if only the candles were lit; but what will happen then? I wonder if the trees from the forest will come to look at me; I wonder if the Sparrows will fly against the pane; shall I grow fast here, or stand thus adorned through winter and summer?" Well, at last, it knew all about it; but it had a real barkache from mere longing, and a barkache is as bad for a tree as a headache is for a human being.

At last the candles were lit. How beautiful! how brilliant it was! And the Tree trembled in all its branches, so that one of the candles set fire to a green twig, and this was really painful. "Oh, dear! oh, dear!" cried the young ladies, putting out the fire as quickly as possible. After this, the tree did not even dare to tremble. It was quite terrified—so much afraid indeed of burning some of its ornaments that it was dazed in the midst of all its splendor.

All at once, the folding-doors were thrown open, and a number of children rushed in as if they intended to overturn the whole Tree. The elders followed more slowly. The little ones stood silent with astonishment, but only for a moment; then they shouted till the room rang, and danced round the Tree, while one present after another was plucked from its branches.

"What are they doing?" thought the Tree; "what is going to happen?" The candles burned down to the twigs, and one after the other they were put out. Then the children were allowed to rifle the Tree. How they rushed at it, so that every branch cracked again; if the top and the tinsel star had not been fastened to the ceiling, the whole Tree would have fallen over. The children danced about with their pretty toys; no one paid any attention to the Tree except an old nurse who peered through the branches, and that was only to see if a fig or an apple had been forgotten.

"A story! a story!" cried the children, drawing a fat little man towards the Tree. He sat down just underneath it. "Here we shall be in the green country," he said, "and the Tree will have the advantage of listening to my story; but I am only going to tell you one. Would you like to hear the history of Ivede Avede, or would you rather hear of Humpty-Dumpty, who fell downstairs, and yet was raised to honor and married the princess?"

"Ivede Avede!" cried some; "Humpty-Dumpty!" cried others; what a screaming there was! Only the Christmas Tree stood silent and pensive. "And am I to do nothing?" it thought; but it had already done all that it was expected to do.

So the man told the story of Humpty-Dumpty, who fell downstairs, and yet came to honor and married the princess; and the children clapped their hands, and cried: "Tell us another! Tell us another!" For they wanted Ivede Avede as well, but they only got the one about Humpty-Dumpty. The Christmas Tree stood quiet and pensive. The birds in the forest had never told such a wonderful story as this, when Humpty-Dumpty fell downstairs and yet married the princess.

"Well, that is the way of the world," thought the Christmas Tree, and it quite believed that the story was true, because the man who told it seemed so very nice.

"Well, who knows," it thought; "perhaps I, too, shall fall downstairs and marry a princess." Meanwhile, it rejoiced to think that it would be decked out the same way next day, with candles and toys, gold, and fruit. "Tomorrow I shall not tremble," it said to itself; "I shall enjoy my grandeur. Tomorrow I shall hear the story of Humpty-Dumpty again, and perhaps Ivede Avede as well"; and the Tree stood quiet and pensive throughout the whole night.

The next morning the man-servant and a maid came in. "Now the fun will start again,"

thought the Tree; but they dragged it out of the room, up the stairs, and into the attic; and there it was put away in a dark corner where no daylight could reach it.

"What does this mean?" thought the Tree; "what am I going to do here; what can I hear up here?" and it leaned against the wall, and thought, and thought. And plenty of time it had to think, for although days and nights went by, nobody came up to the attic, and when at last somebody came, it was only to put away some big boxes in the corner.

The Tree was now quite hidden, and it appeared to be forgotten. "Well, it is winter outdoors," it thought; "the earth is hard and covered with snow, and the people cannot plant me now; I shall, therefore, have to stand here until the spring. How considerate that is! How kind people really are! If only it were not so dark here, and so fearfully lonely; there is not even a little hare. It really was nice out in the forest, when the ground was covered with snow, and the hare ran by—yes, even when he jumped over me, although at the time I did not like it. Up here it is terribly lonely."

"Peep, peep," said a little Mouse, as it crept forth. Then came another, which sniffed at the Fir Tree and slipped in amongst its branches. "It is awfully cold," said the little Mouse, "or else it would be very nice in here. Don't you think so, old Fir Tree?"

"I am not at all old," said the Fir Tree; "there are many much older than I."

"Where do you come from?" asked the Mice, "and what do you know?" They were terribly inquisitive. "Now tell us about the most beautiful spot on earth—have you been there? Have you been into the pantry, where cheese is lying on the shelves and the hams are hanging from the ceiling, where one dances on tallow-candles—where one goes in thin and comes out fat?"

"I don't know about that," said the Tree, "but I know the forest, where the sun shines and the birds sing," and then it told its whole history from youth upwards.

The little Mice had never heard of such things before, and they listened and said: "Oh! how many things you have seen! How happy you have been!"

"I?" said the Fir Tree, and it thought over what it had said. "Well, as a matter of fact, it *was* rather jolly at times." And then it told about the Christmas Eve, when it was dressed with cakes and candles.

"Ah!" said the little Mice, "you have indeed been happy, old Fir Tree."

"I am not at all old," said the Tree; "it was only this winter that I came from the forest. I am in the prime of life and am only stunted in my growth."

"What nice tales he can tell!" said the little Mice.

And the next night four more little Mice came in to hear the Fir Tree's stories, and the more it told, the better it remembered everything, and began to think they had been very splendid times! But they might come again, for did not Humpty-Dumpty fall downstairs and yet marry the princess?

"Perhaps," it said to itself, "I also may marry a princess"; and it thought of the pretty little Birch Tree that grew out in the forest, for the Birch was to the Fir Tree a real little princess.

"Who is Humpty-Dumpty?" asked the little Mice. And the Tree told them the fairy tale from beginning to end. It remembered every single word, and the little Mice were ready to run up to the top of the Tree for pure joy. Next night a great many more Mice came in, and on Sunday two Rats; but in their opinion the story was not funny. The little Mice were very sorry for this, and they, too, began to think less of it.

"Do you know only that one story?" asked the Rats.

"Only that one," said the Tree. "It was the story I heard on my happiest, happiest evening; but I did not know then how happy I was."

"It is a very poor story. Don't you know anything about bacon or tallow candles—do you know no pantry stories?"

"No," said the Tree.

"Well, then, we don't want to hear from you," said the Rats, so they went home.

At last the little Mice also went home, and the Tree sighed.

"It was very nice when those merry little Mice were sitting around me, listening to what I told them. Now that also is past, but I shall know how to amuse myself when I am taken out again."

But when did this happen? Well, one morning some people came and rummaged about in the garret; the boxes were moved, and the Tree was taken out; they threw it rather roughly on the floor, and soon a man dragged it down towards the staircase, where the daylight shone in. "Now life begins again," thought the Tree, as it felt the fresh air and the first sunbeam. Then it found itself out in the yard; but all this happened so quickly that the Tree altogether forgot to look at itself—there was so much to see all around it. The yard adjoined the garden, where everything was in bloom; roses, fresh and fragrant, hung over the little paling, the linden-trees were blooming, and the Swallows flew about and cried: "Tweet, tweet! my husband has come." But it was not the Fir Tree that they meant.

"Now I am going to live," cried the Fir Tree joyously, and it spread out its branches; but lo! they were all withered and yellow, and lay in a corner amongst weeds and nettles. The tinsel star still stuck at the top of the Tree, glittering in the bright sunshine.

In the yard two merry children were playing. They had danced round the tree at Christmas-time and greatly enjoyed themselves. The smaller of the two ran up and tore off the tinsel star. "Look what is still sticking to that ugly old Christmas Tree!" he said, and trod on the branches so that they cracked under his boots.

The Tree looked at all the beauty of the flowers and the freshness of the garden; then it looked at itself, and wished that it had been left in its dark corner in the garret. It thought of its fresh youth in the forest, of the merry Christmas Eve, and of the little Mice that were so glad to listen to the story of Humpty-Dumpty.

"All is over!" said the poor Tree; "if only I had enjoyed myself when I could have done so! But it is all over now!" And the man-servant came and chopped the Tree up into little pieces, until there was a whole bundle of it. The man-servant lit a match, and the Fir Tree blazed brightly under the great copper, and it sighed deeply, every sigh sounding like a tiny pistol-shot. The children who were playing came in and sat down in front of the fire, looked into it, and cried: "Piff! paff!" but at each shot there was a deep sigh. It was the Tree, thinking of the summer day in the wood, of the winter night when the stars were shining, of Christmas Eve, and of Humpty-Dumpty, the only fairy tale it had ever heard, or could tell.

And so the Tree was burned to ashes. The children played in the yard, and the little one pinned on his breast the tinsel star that the Tree had worn on its happiest evening.

Now it was all over—the Tree was gone, and the story with it. And this is the way of all stories.

A HOME FOR TANDY

By Audrey and Harvey Hirsch
Illustrated by Tim and Greg Hildebrandt

ALL over the green meadows and deep in the cool forest, everything was still. The little folk of Twinbrook Hollow were fast asleep. Some were curled snugly in hollow logs while others dozed in tall trees high above the forest floor. Under one of these tall trees, Tandy, a tiny elf, lay sleeping.

Soon the first ray of morning sunshine danced across Tandy's nose. He sat straight up and rubbed his eyes. Sniffing the cool, clear air, he felt that winter must be very close. Yes, very close indeed!

"Snow and ice will soon cover the forest," he thought. "Today I MUST find a warm, dry home."

But now Tandy was growing hungry. With a small basket swinging from his hand, he skipped through a meadow and onto the autumn forest's well-worn path.

Ahead of him, on the forest's edge, he could see a row of blackberry bushes. This was a happy sight. Tandy liked blackberries better than anything! He hurried to the first bush.

Stretching as straight and tall as a wee elf can stretch, he reached for a round, juicy berry. Tandy tugged and tugged! Down bumped a berry.

"Mmmmm . . . this is delicious," munched Tandy.

"It certainly is!" spoke a voice from behind the bush. At that moment the owner of the voice appeared. He wore a small black mask.

"Good morning, Raccoon," said Tandy. "Last time we met, you were catching fish down at the pond."

"Yes, that was only a few days ago and already it is too cool to wade in the water. Winter days will soon be here," said Raccoon.

"I do hope I'll have a warm home before winter comes. I have been looking and looking, but I'm really not sure what kind of home I'm looking for," sighed Tandy.

"My home is very cozy in winter," said Raccoon. "Maybe you could move in with me. Come on, I'll show it to you."

Tandy popped a blackberry into his basket and followed Raccoon.

Soon they reached the foot of a tall maple tree.

"Well, there it is," said Raccoon, pointing up to a hole in a big, bent branch. "Follow me," he called, as he scampered up to his house.

"I'd like to, but I'm afraid I can't climb a tree," answered Tandy.

"Oh, dear," said Raccoon, looking down at the tiny elf, "I guess a house like mine isn't good for you after all."

Tandy said good-bye and started sadly on his way. He had never felt sad before, not even when his mushroom house rolled away during the big windstorm. It was summer then, and playing in the sun, finding berries, and sleeping out under the stars on the cool grass was fun. But things were different now. Winter was coming. The cold nights made Tandy shiver. And during the cool days his friends were busy getting ready for the colder days ahead.

"I have to get ready, too," said Tandy, as he walked quickly down the path. "Somewhere there MUST be a home where an elf can live."

Passing a grassy bank, Tandy spied a hole. He skipped up to it and peered down into the darkness. Lying on his tummy and pushing with his toes, Tandy scooted a little further into the doorway to get a better look.

Suddenly he was rolling down a long, dark tunnel. Head over heels he rolled. After nine dizzy somersaults, he bumped against something soft and furry.

"Goodness me!" said the furry something. "Who is in my house?"

"I'm sorry," sputtered Tandy. "I didn't know anyone lived here. I was just looking for a winter home. I hope I didn't bump you too hard. My name is Tandy, and after nine somersaults, I feel a little dizzy."

"Well, well, so you're Tandy. Muskrat has told me about you. I'm Mole. I was just digging out a new kitchen. How do you like it?" asked the Mole in his slow, quiet voice.

"Uh—well, I'm sure it is very nice, but I can't see it. It's so dark down here I can't see anything," stammered Tandy.

"That's funny," replied Mole. "I never noticed that."

Mole went on digging and Tandy slowly crawled up the tunnel. The sharp stones hurt his knees and the soft dirt made him sneeze.

Out in the clear air again, he brushed the dirt from his cinnamon-red jacket.

"That's just not a good home for an elf," thought Tandy, blinking at the bright sunlight. Tandy climbed down a grassy slope to the edge of the old pond. He cupped his tiny hands and filled them with water. It tasted cool and good. He took a long drink and then washed his tiny face.

"It might be nice to live near here," thought Tandy.

Just then, a wet, brown head bobbed out of the water.

"Hi there, Tandy!" said Beaver. "What are you doing down this way?"

"I'm just resting a little and getting a drink," replied Tandy. "You see, I'm looking for a winter home that is just right for me. It seems that each home I look at is either not right for me or I'm not right for it. I'm terrible at climbing trees, and tunnels mix me up."

"Maybe I can help you," said Beaver. "My home is just right. If you like it, I'll help you build one. What do you think?"

"That sounds very nice," said Tandy hopefully.

Beaver pointed to a pile of branches and dried grass in the middle of the old pond.

"Jump on my back, hold on tight, and we will soon be there."

Swiftly, Beaver swam through the water with Tandy holding tight. Just before they reached the pile of branches and dried grass, Beaver dove down under the water, through an opening, and up into his house. There on a dry ledge, he dropped Tandy.

"Well!" said Beaver. "What do you think of it?"

But Tandy couldn't answer—he was too busy trying to catch his breath. His tiny ears and nose were filled with water. First he coughed and then he sneezed. Tandy lay on the ledge, shivering. He was terribly frightened. Beaver was terribly sorry.

"Oh, Tandy, I forgot that elves can't go diving under water."

When Tandy was dry, Beaver helped him squeeze between the branches to the roof of his house. There he waited for Beaver to give him a ride back to the grassy bank.

"Good-bye, Tandy," said Beaver. "I'm sorry I couldn't help you."

Tandy said good-bye to Beaver and once more set out to find a winter home.

All day long he looked for a home where a tiny elf could live. Once he found a dark cave where a bat slept hanging upside down.

"I wonder if I could do that," thought Tandy.

Bump! Thump! Down came Tandy.

"How curious," said a surprised Tandy, rubbing his tiny head. "I wonder how bats do it!"

Later, Tandy found a bug village at the bottom of a dried sunflower stalk. But he was too big to fit into any of the tiny houses.

By this time Tandy was becoming tired, so tired he could walk no farther. He sat down on the ground and leaned back against the sunflower stalk. A tear rolled down his cheek, then another, and still another, until the tips of his shoes were all wet. A little sigh came from the bottom of the sunflower stalk, and soon Tandy was fast asleep.

But while Tandy slept, a meeting was being held on the flat rock at the edge of the forest. All Tandy's friends were there, and they were all chattering at once. Beaver was there and so was Mole, and Raccoon, too. Each told the other animals how Tandy had tried to find a home.

"It's too bad," said Raccoon, "but he just isn't a climber."

"Nice elf," muttered Mole quietly, "but he has a problem. Can't see in the dark. Very strange, very strange!"

Then Beaver declared that Tandy was definitely not suited for underwater living.

"Well, now, this is very serious," said Owl. "Tandy is without a home and winter is almost here. We must find a home that is just right for an elf."

So everyone thought and thought and thought.

Suddenly, Robin clapped her wings. "I know! I know!" she chirped. "In winter I always fly south where it is warmer. Tandy could go with me!"

Everyone chattered excitedly.

"Quiet! Quiet!" hooted Owl. "That won't do. We want Tandy to stay here with his friends. Let me think."

Owl closed his eyes. Everyone was quiet, hoping that Owl would be able to solve Tandy's problem.

"A-HA!" cried Owl. "I have it! If none of *our* homes is quite right for Tandy, then we must build one that is! But we must get busy, for we haven't much time before nightfall. Now here is my plan."

The animals moved closer, listening eagerly to Owl's instructions.

"Beaver, you have the strongest teeth. Cut a pile of sticks for the walls. Sparrow, you gather straw for the roof. Squirrels, you gather nutshells and acorn tops for dishes and bowls." Then Owl turned to the rest of the animals. "Now, the rest of you—we all have things to do. There is furniture to be made and food to gather. So, let's get busy!"

What a hustling and bustling there was. Walls went up, a roof went on, a moss carpet was laid down. Cupboards were built to hold the supply of berries and nuts the squirrels and chipmunks had gathered.

The Fieldmouse Twins carried in a large mushroom for a table and placed four small toadstools around it. Crow brought a milkweed pod filled with soft white down for Tandy's bed. Spider spun lacy curtains for the windows.

Just as the sun slipped silently down the other side of the mountain, the last acorn chair was placed inside the tiny house. All the happy, tired animals felt very proud as they stood before the finished house.

Robin was sent to fetch Tandy. When Tandy appeared, all the animals cheered. He stood in front of the little house and rubbed his eyes again and again.

"Oh, what a lovely home," he murmured.

"It's yours, it's yours," the animals chorused.

Tandy was so happy that he could barely whisper a small thank you. But to the animals of Twinbrook Hollow, this was more than enough.

That night Tandy asked the fireflies in his new lamp to put out their lights. Then he tucked the soft, silky milkweed up under his chin, snuggled deeper into his warm bed and closed his eyes in happy sleep.

Winter arrived that same night. The first snowflakes floated softly to the ground, but Tandy did not see them. He was fast asleep in his new home.

SLEEPING BEAUTY
Illustrated by Eulalie

A KING and a Queen once reigned in a country a great way off, where there were in those days fairies. Now this King and Queen had plenty of money, and plenty of fine clothes and good things to eat and drink, but though they had been married many years, they had no children, and this grieved them very much indeed.

One day as the Queen was walking by the side of the river, she saw a poor little fish that had thrown itself out of the water and lay gasping and nearly dead on the bank. The Queen took pity on the little fish and threw it back again into the river; and before it swam away, it lifted its head out of the water and said, "I know what your wish is, and it shall be fulfilled. In return for your kindness to me, you will soon have a daughter."

What the little fish had foretold soon came to pass; and the Queen had a beautiful little girl. The King announced that he would hold a great feast to show the child to all the people in his land. So he invited his kinsmen, and nobles, and friends, and neighbors. But the Queen said, "I will have the fairies, also, that they might be kind and good to our little daughter."

Now there were thirteen fairies in the kingdom; but since the King and Queen had only twelve golden dishes, they were forced to leave one of the fairies without inviting her.

So the twelve fairies came, each with a high red cap on her head, red shoes with high heels on her feet, and a long white wand in her hand; and after the feast was over, they gathered round in a ring and gave all their best gifts to the little Princess. One gave her goodness, another beauty, another riches, and so on till she had all that was good in the world.

Just as the eleventh had given her blessing, a great noise was heard in the courtyard and word was brought that the thirteenth fairy had come, with a black cap on her head, black shoes on her feet, and a broomstick in her hand; and presently she entered the dining-room. Now, since she had not been asked to the feast, she was very angry, and scolding the King and Queen, she set to work to take her revenge. She cried out, "The King's daughter shall, in her fifteenth year, be wounded by a spindle and fall down dead."

The whole company was horrified by the terrible prophesy. Then the twelfth of the friendly fairies, who had not yet given her gift, came forward and said that the evil wish must be fulfilled, but that she could soften its mischief. So her gift was that the King's daughter, when the spindle wounded her, should not really die, but should only fall asleep for one hundred years.

However, the King hoped still to save his dear child altogether from the threatened evil; so he ordered that all the spindles in the kingdom should be burnt.

As the Princess grew, all the gifts of the first eleven fairies were fulfilled, for the Princess was so beautiful, well-behaved, good, and wise that everyone who knew her loved her.

It happened that, on the very day she was fifteen years old, the King and Queen were busily preparing a party in the Princess's honor, and she was left alone in the palace. So she roamed about by herself and looked at all the rooms and chambers, till at last she came to an old tower to which there was a narrow staircase ending with a little door. In the door there was a golden key, and when she turned it, the door sprang open. There sat an old lady spinning away very busily.

"Why, good woman," said the Princess; "what are you doing there?"

"Spinning," said the old lady, and nodded her head, humming a tune, while buzz! went the wheel.

"How prettily that little thing turns round!" said the Princess, and she took the spindle and began to try it. But scarcely had she touched it before the fairy's prophecy was fulfilled; the spindle wounded her, and she fell down lifeless on the ground.

However, she was not dead, but had only fallen into a deep sleep; and as she slept, the King and Queen and all their court fell asleep, too. Even the cooks who were preparing the birthday feast slumbered over their sauces and sweetmeats. And the horses slept in the stables, and the dogs in the court, the pigeons on the housetop, and the flies slept upon the walls.

A large hedge of thorns soon grew round the palace, and every year it became higher and thicker, till at last the old palace was surrounded and hidden so that not even the roof or the chimneys could be seen. But word spread through all the land of the beautiful Sleeping Beauty (for so the King's daughter was called)—so that, from time to time, princes came and tried to break through the thicket into the palace. This, however, none of them could ever do.

After many, many years there came a king's son into that land, and an old man told him the story of the thicket of thorns, and how a beautiful palace stood behind it, and how a wonderful Princess, called Sleeping Beauty, lay in it asleep with all her court.

Then the young Prince said, "I shall go and see this Sleeping Beauty."

Now that very day the hundred years were ended, and as the Prince came to the thicket, he saw nothing but beautiful flowering shrubs, through which he went with ease, and they shut in after him as thick as ever.

Then he came to the palace, and there in the court lay the dogs asleep; and the horses were standing in the stables; and on the roof sat the pigeons fast asleep, with their heads under their wings.

And when he came into the palace, the flies were sleeping on the walls; the spit was standing still; the butler had a jug of ale to his lips, going to drink a draught; and the maid sat with a fowl in her lap ready to be plucked.

Then he went on still farther, and all was so still that he could hear every breath he drew; till at last he came to the old tower. He opened the door of the little room, and there was Sleeping Beauty, fast asleep on a couch by the window. She looked so beautiful that he could not take his eyes off her, so he stooped down and gave her a kiss. The moment he kissed her, she opened her eyes and awoke. And, at the same time, the King and Queen also awoke, and all the court, and gazed on one another with great wonder. And the horses shook themselves; and the dogs jumped up and barked; the pigeons took their heads from under their wings and flew into the fields; the flies on the walls buzzed again; the fire in the kitchen blazed up; round went the jack, and round went the spit, with the goose for the King's dinner upon it.

As soon as Sleeping Beauty saw the Prince she fell immediately in love with him. And he, of course, was already deeply in love with her. So they were married, and a wedding feast was given. And they lived happily together all their lives long.

THE THREE BILLY GOATS GRUFF

Illustrated by Tasha Tudor

ONCE upon a time there were three billy goats who wanted to go up to the hillside to eat the green grass there and make themselves fat. And the name of all the three billy goats was "Gruff."

On the way up to the hillside was a bridge over a stream, and under the bridge lived a great big ugly Troll, with eyes as big as dinner plates and a nose as long as a poker.

So first of all the youngest billy goat Gruff came to the stream and started to cross the bridge.

Trip, Trap, Trip, Trap, went the bridge, for the little billy goat Gruff was not very heavy. And the great big ugly Troll roared out:

"Who's that tripping over my bridge?"

"Oh, it's only me, the smallest billy goat Gruff. I want to go up to the hillside to eat grass and make myself fat," said the youngest billy goat in his tiny voice.

"Wait, I'm coming to gobble you up," said the Troll.

"Oh, no, don't eat me, I'm much too little. The second billy goat Gruff is coming right behind me, and he's much bigger than I am," said the youngest billy goat Gruff.

"Oh, very well then, be off with you," said the Troll.

Then the second billy goat Gruff came up to the stream and started to cross the bridge.

TRIP, TRAP, TRIP, TRAP, went the bridge, for the middle-sized billy goat Gruff was fairly heavy. And the great big ugly Troll roared out:

"Who's that tripping over my bridge?"

"OH, IT'S ONLY ME, THE SECOND BILLY GOAT GRUFF. I WANT TO GO UP TO THE HILLSIDE TO EAT GRASS AND MAKE MYSELF FAT," said the second billy goat Gruff in a middle-sized voice.

"Wait, I'm coming to gobble you up," said the Troll.

"OH, NO, DON'T EAT ME, I'M ONLY MIDDLE-SIZED. THE BIG BILLY GOAT GRUFF IS COMING RIGHT BEHIND ME, AND HE'S MUCH BIGGER THAN I AM," said the second billy goat Gruff.

"Oh, very well then, be off with you," said the Troll.

And so a little while later, the big billy goat Gruff came up to the stream and started to cross the bridge.

TRIP, TRAP, TRIP, TRAP, went the bridge, for the big billy goat Gruff was very heavy.

"Who's that tripping over my bridge?" roared the great big ugly Troll.

"OH, IT'S ONLY ME, THE BIG BILLY GOAT GRUFF. WHAT DO YOU WANT?" said the big billy goat Gruff in a very loud voice.

"Wait, I'm coming to gobble you up," said the Troll.

"COME ON UP," said the big billy goat Gruff. "I'M NOT AFRAID OF YOU."

Up climbed the Troll from under the bridge, and the big billy goat Gruff put his big head down and ran at the Troll with his big horns. "BUMP" went the big billy goat Gruff. And "Splash" went the great ugly Troll, right into the water. And he was never heard of again.

So the three billy goats Gruff went up to the hillside together. There they ate grass and grew fat and lived happily ever after.

LITTLE BLACK SAMBO

By Helen Bannerman

Illustrated by Eulalie

ONCE upon a time a little boy lived in India, and his name was Little Black Sambo. And his mother was called Mama Sari. And his father was called Papa Simbu.

And Mama Sari made him a beautiful red coat and a pair of beautiful little blue trousers.

And Papa Simbu went to the bazaar and bought him a beautiful green umbrella and a lovely little pair of purple shoes with crimson soles and crimson linings.

And then wasn't Little Black Sambo grand? So he put on all his fine clothes and went out for a walk in the jungle. And by and by he met a tiger. And the tiger said to him, "Little Black Sambo, I'm going to eat you up!"

And Little Black Sambo said, "Oh! Please, Mr. Tiger, don't eat me up. I'll give you my beautiful little red coat."

So the tiger said, "Very well, I won't eat you this time." And it took poor Little Black Sambo's beautiful little red coat, and it went away, saying, "Now I'm the grandest tiger in the jungle."

And Little Black Sambo went on, and by and by he met another tiger, and it said to him, "Little Black Sambo, I'm going to eat you up!"

And Little Black Sambo said, "Oh! Please, Mr. Tiger, don't eat me up. I'll give you my beautiful blue trousers."

So the tiger said, "Very well, I won't eat you this time." And it took poor Little Black Sambo's beautiful blue trousers and went away saying, "Now I'm the grandest tiger in the jungle."

And Little Black Sambo went on, and by and by he met another tiger, and it said to him, "Little Black Sambo, I'm going to eat you up!"

And Little Black Sambo said, "Oh! Please, Mr. Tiger, don't eat me up. I'll give you my beautiful little purple shoes with crimson soles and crimson linings."

But the tiger said, "What use would your shoes be to me? I have four feet, and you've only two. You haven't enough shoes for me."

And Little Black Sambo said, "You could wear them on your ears."

"So I could," said the tiger. "That's a very good idea. Give them to me, and I won't eat you this time." So he took poor Little Black Sambo's beautiful little purple shoes with crimson soles and crimson linings and went away, saying, "Now I'm the grandest tiger in the jungle."

And by and by Little Black Sambo met another tiger, and it said to him, "Little Black Sambo, I'm going to eat you up!"

And Little Black Sambo said, "Oh! Please, Mr. Tiger, don't eat me up. I'll give you my beautiful green umbrella."

But the tiger said, "How can I carry an umbrella when I need all my paws for walking?"

"You could tie it on your tail and carry it that way," said Little Black Sambo.

"So I could," said the tiger. "Give it to me, and I won't eat you this time." So he took poor Little Black Sambo's beautiful green umbrella and went away, saying, "Now I'm the grandest tiger in the jungle."

And poor Little Black Sambo went away crying, because the tigers had taken all his fine clothes.

Presently, he heard a horrible noise that sounded like "G-r-r-rrrrrr,"and it grew louder and louder. "Oh, dear!" said Little Black Sambo. "All the tigers are coming back to eat me up!" So he ran to a palm tree and peeped around—and there he saw all the tigers arguing over which of them was the grandest. They all became so angry that they jumped up and took off the fine clothes and began to tear each other with their claws and bite each other with their big white teeth.

And they came rolling and tumbling to the foot of the very tree where Little Black Sambo was hiding, but he jumped quickly away behind another tree. And the tigers all caught hold of each other's tails, and they wrangled and scrambled.

And soon they found themselves in a ring around the tree.

Then Little Black Sambo jumped up and called out, "Oh, tigers! Why have you taken off all your nice clothes? Don't you want them?"

But the tigers only answered, "G-r-r-rrrrr!"

Then Little Black Sambo said, "If you want them, say so, or I'll take them back."

But the tigers would not let go of each other's tails, so they could only say, "G-r-r-rrrr!"

So Little Black Sambo put on all his fine clothes again.

And the tigers became very, very angry, but still they would not let go of each other's tails. And they became so angry that they ran around the tree, trying to eat each other up.

And they ran faster and faster, till they were whirling so fast Little Black Sambo couldn't see their legs at all.

And still they ran faster and faster, till they all just melted away, and there was nothing left but a great big pool of melted butter round the foot of the tree.

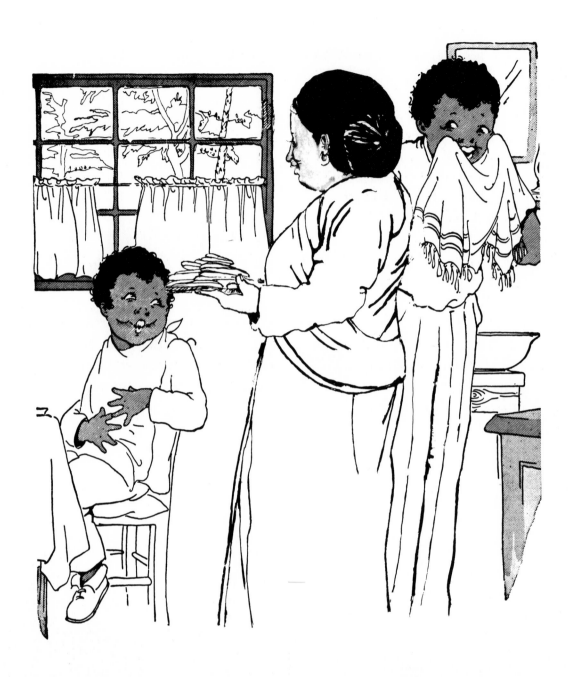

Now, Papa Simbu was just coming home from work with a great big brass pot in his arms, and when he saw what was left of the tigers he said, "Oh! What lovely melted butter!"

So he put it all into the great big brass pot and took it home to Mama Sari.

When Mama Sari saw the melted butter, wasn't she pleased! "Now," she said, "we'll all have pancakes for supper!"

So Mama Sari made pancake batter. And she fried it in the melted butter which the tigers had made, and out came pancakes just as yellow and brown as little tigers.

And then they all sat down to supper. And Mama Sari ate twenty-seven pancakes, and Papa Simbu ate fifty-five, but Little Black Sambo ate one hundred and sixty-three, because he was so hungry!

THE GOOSEGIRL

Illustrated by Eulalie

THERE once was an old Queen whose husband had been dead for many years, and she had a very beautiful daughter who was betrothed to a Prince in a distant country. Although she loved her daughter dearly, the Queen was too old to accompany her daughter on the long journey. So she sent a Waiting-woman to travel with her and to put the Princess's hand into that of the bridegroom. This Waiting-woman was very strong that she might protect and care for the Princess. The Queen gave to each a horse; the Princess's horse was called Falada, and it could speak.

When the hour of departure came, the Princess mounted her horse and set out for her bridegroom's country. When they had ridden for a time, the Princess became very thirsty and said to the Waiting-woman, "Get down and fetch me some water in my cup from the stream. I must have something to drink."

"If you are thirsty," said the Waiting-woman, "dismount yourself, lie down by the water and drink. I don't choose to be your servant." So, in her great thirst, the Princess dismounted and stooped down to the stream and drank, since she was not to have her golden cup.

Now, when she was about to mount Falada, the Waiting-woman said, "Falada belongs to me now; this jade will do for you!"

The poor little Princess protested, but she was obliged to give way. Then the Waiting-woman, in a harsh voice, ordered her to take off her royal robes and to put on the servant's own mean garments. Finally, she forced her to swear before heaven that she would not tell a creature at the court what had taken place. If she would not take the oath, she would be killed on the spot. But Falada saw all this. The Waiting-woman then mounted Falada and put the real bride on her poor jade, and they continued their journey.

There was great rejoicing when they arrived at the castle. The Prince hurried towards them and lifted the Waiting-woman from her horse, thinking she was his bride. She was led upstairs, but the real Princess had to stay below. The old King looked out of the window and saw the delicate, pretty little creature standing in the courtyard, so he arranged that she might help a little lad named Conrad who looked after the geese.

Soon after, the false bride said to the husband-to-be, "Dear Prince, I pray you to do me a favor."

He answered, "That will I gladly."

"Well, then, let the knacker be called to cut off the head of the horse I rode; it angered me on the way."

Really, she was afraid that the horse would speak, and tell of her treatment of the Princess. And so it was settled that the faithful Falada would die.

When this came to the ear of the real Princess, she promised the knacker a piece of gold if he would do her a service. There was a great dark gateway to the town, through which she had to pass every morning and evening. "Will you nail up Falada's head in this gateway so that I might see him as I pass?" she asked.

The knacker promised to do as she wished, and when the horse's head was cut off, he hung it up in the dark gateway. In the early morning, when she and Conrad went through the gateway, she said in passing—"Alas! dear Falada, there thou hangest." And the Head answered—"Alas! Queen's daughter, there thou gangest. If thy mother knew thy fate, her heart would break with grief so great."

Then they passed on out of the town, right into the fields with the geese. And they tended the geese till the evening. When they got home, Conrad went to the old King and said, "I won't tend the geese with that maiden again. She frightens me."

When the old King then ordered him to say what she did to frighten him, Conrad said,

"In the morning, when we passed under the dark gateway with the geese, she talked to a horse's head, which is hung up on the wall. She said—'Alas! dear Falada, there thou hangest,' and the Head answered—'Alas! Queen's daughter, there thou gangest. If thy mother knew thy fate, her heart would break with grief so great.'"

The old King ordered Conrad to go out the next day as usual. Then he placed himself behind the dark gateway and heard the Princess speaking to Falada's head. Thereupon he went away unnoticed; and in the evening, when the Goosegirl came home, he called her aside and asked why she did all this.

"That I may not tell you, nor may I tell any human creature; for I have sworn it under the open sky, because if I had not done so, I should have lost my life."

He gave her no peace, but she would not break her oath. Then he said, "If you won't tell me, then tell your sorrows to the iron stove there," and he went away.

So she crept up to the stove and, beginning to weep and lament, unburdened her heart to it saying, "Here I am, forsaken by all the world, and yet I am a Princess. A false Waiting-woman brought me to such a pass that I had to take off my royal robes. Then she took my place with my bridegroom, while I have to do mean service as a Goosegirl. If my mother knew, it would break her heart."

The old King stood outside by the pipes of the stove and heard all that she said. Then he came back, had royal robes put upon her, and called his son. He told him that he had a false bride who was only a Waiting-woman; the true bride was the Goosegirl.

The young Prince was charmed by her youth and beauty, and a great banquet was prepared to which all the courtiers and good friends were bidden. The bridegroom sat at the head of the table, with the Princess on one side and the Waiting-woman on the other; but the Waiting-woman was so dazzled that she did not recognize the Princess.

When they had eaten and drunk and were all very merry, the old King put a riddle to the Waiting-woman. "What does a person deserve who deceives his master?"

The false bride answered, "He must be put stark naked into a barrel stuck with nails and made to walk through the streets until he starves."

"Then that is your own doom," said the King, "and the judgment shall be carried out."

When the sentence was fulfilled, the young Prince married his true bride, and they ruled their kingdom together in peace and happiness.

THE STORY OF CHICKEN LITTLE

Illustrated by Margaret Campbell Hoopes

ONCE upon a time, there was a dear little chicken named Chicken Little. And although she was very small, with hardly any neck at all, somehow she always found her legs were long enough to reach the ground.

Chicken Little liked to watch the sun paint lovely colors in the sky outside her cottage just before bedtime.

One day as she was scratching for corn in her garden, a pebble fell off the roof and hit her on the head.

"Oh, dear me!" she cried, "the sky is falling. I must go and tell the King."

And away she ran, down the road.

By and by she met Henny Penny going to the store.

"Where are you going?" asked Henny Penny.

"I'm going to tell the King the sky is falling," answered Chicken Little.

"How do you know the sky is falling?" asked Henny Penny.

"Because a piece of it fell on my head," said Chicken Little.

"May I go with you?" begged Henny Penny.

"Certainly," answered Chicken Little.

She hastened on, followed by Henny Penny.

Turning up a shady lane they met Ducky Daddles.

"Where are you two going?" asked Ducky Daddles.

80

"We are going to tell the King the sky is falling," answered Henny Penny.

"How do you know?" asked Ducky Daddles.

"Chicken Little told me," said Henny Penny.

"A piece of it fell on my head," cried Chicken Little.

"May I go with you?" asked Ducky Daddles.

"Certainly," answered Chicken Little.

Then away went Chicken Little, Henny Penny and Ducky Daddles.

By and by they passed the farmyard where Goosie Poosie was talking to Piggy Wiggy. When she saw them hurrying by she asked:

"Where are you three going?"

"The sky is falling and we are going to tell the King," answered Ducky Daddles.

"How do you know?" asked Goosie Poosie.

"Henny Penny told me," said Ducky Daddles.

"Chicken Little told me," said Henny Penny.

"A piece of it fell on my head," Chicken Little cried.

"May I go with you?" asked Goosie Poosie.

"Certainly," said Chicken Little.

So off they all started again.

By and by whom should they meet but Turkey Lurkey, who had just been talking to Bunny Rabbit, was strutting along the lane.

"Where are you four going?" he asked.

"The sky is falling and we are going to tell the King," answered Goosie Poosie.

"How do you know?" asked Turkey Lurkey.

"Ducky Daddles told me," said Goosie Poosie.

"Henny Penny told me," said Ducky Daddles.

"Chicken Little told me," said Henny Penny.

"A piece of it fell on my head," cried Chicken Little.

"May I go with you?" asked Turkey Lurkey.

"Certainly," said Chicken Little.

Then Turkey Lurkey followed Chicken Little, Henny Penny, Ducky Daddles and Goosie Poosie.

On and on they went along the road that led to the castle of the King.

But as they went along Foxy Loxy saw them, and came creeping through the woods after them. All the while he was licking his lips, thinking what a fine meal each of them would make.

Suddenly out from behind a bush he jumped and said very politely, "Where are you all going?"

"Why, Foxy Loxy, don't you know the sky is falling? We are going to tell the King," they all replied at once.

"How do you know?" asked Foxy Loxy.

"Goosie Poosie told me," said Turkey Lurkey.

"Ducky Daddles told me," said Goosie Poosie.

"Henny Penny told me," said Ducky Daddles.

"Chicken Little told me," said Henny Penny.

"A piece of it fell on my head," cried Chicken Little.

"Oh! But this is not the way to the King, Chicken Little, Henny Penny, Ducky Daddles, Goosie Poosie and Turkey Lurkey. I know the proper way; shall I show it to you?" asked Foxy Loxy.

"Oh, certainly," they all answered at once. So Chicken Little, Henny Penny, Ducky Daddles, Goosie Poosie and Turkey Lurkey all followed Foxy Loxy.

He led them along until they reached the door of his house.

"This is a short way to the King's Palace; you'll soon get there if you follow me. I will go in first and call you one at a time, as the way is narrow," said Foxy Loxy.

"Why of course," said Chicken Little.

"Certainly," said Henny Penny.

"Without doubt," said Ducky Daddles.

"Why not?" asked Goosie Poosie.

"Me first," said Turkey Lurkey.

Then Foxy Loxy called Turkey Lurkey, who came in and closed the door. Foxy Loxy caught him, but just as he was about to put him in the pot, Turkey Lurkey flew up in the air and out of a window.

Home he ran as fast as he could go, and he never told the King the sky was falling.

Next Foxy Loxy called Goosie Poosie, who came in and closed the door. Foxy Loxy caught her by the neck, but just as he was about to put her in the pot, she flew up in the air and out the window.

Home she ran as fast as she could go, and she never told the King the sky was falling.

Next Foxy Loxy called Ducky Daddles, who came in and closed the door. Foxy Loxy caught her by the neck, but just as he was about to put her in the pot, she flew up in the air and out of the window.

Home she ran as fast as she could go, and she never told the King the sky was falling.

Then Foxy Loxy called Henny Penny, who came in and closed the door. Foxy Loxy caught her by the neck, but just as he was about to put her in the pot, she flew up in the air and out of the window.

Home she ran as fast as she could go, and she never told the King the sky was falling.

When Chicken Little saw Turkey Lurkey, Goosie Poosie, Ducky Daddles and Henny Penny flying out the window and running home, she became worried. She knew Foxy Loxy was up to some mischief.

When a little chicken is worried she scratches her head. When Chicken Little scratched her head she felt something hard in the feathers and picked it out and looked at it. It was the pebble that had fallen off the roof.

"How silly I am," she said. "This is not a piece of the sky at all, just a pebble off my roof. I don't think the sky was falling. And I don't have to tell the King."

So she went happily back to her cottage. And to this day she has never seen Foxy Loxy again.

And so from this story you'll all agree that it is not safe to follow the advice of strangers, not even if they are polite.

THE LITTLE TURTLE THAT COULD
NOT STOP TALKING

Illustrated by Lucille W. and H. C. Holling

LITTLE Green Turtle lived in a muddy little pond, far across the seas in a country called India. Little Green Turtle liked to swim about in his muddy pond. He liked, too, to crawl out on a flat rock and sun himself.

But best of all Little Green Turtle liked to talk. He talked to the little children who came from the village nearby to play in the pond. He talked to the silvery fish that darted like streaks of light through the water. He talked to the green frogs who answered only, "Kerchunk, kerchunk."

He talked to the long-legged heron that stood in the pond and wondered how Little Green Turtle found so much to say. He talked to Friend Monkey who swung himself about in the treetops. He even chattered faster than Friend Monkey could, and that was saying a good deal.

In fact Little Green Turtle talked to everything that walked or swam, or hopped, or flew or climbed. He talked, talked, talked all the time except when he was asleep.

One day two strong young geese flew by and stopped to rest at the pond. As soon as Little Green Turtle saw them, he called out: "Where are you going, friends?"

"We are going to our home in the South," answered the White Goose.

"And what is your home like?" asked Little Green Turtle.

"Our home is near a beautiful pool in the South," answered the Gray Goose. "Our pool is much larger than your pond. And it is as blue as the sky and as clear as glass."

"Wouldn't you like to go South and see our beautiful pool?" said the White Goose.

"Yes, indeed," answered Little Green Turtle. "I have always wanted to go South, but how can I go? I have no strong wings like yours. I cannot fly, so I can only stay here, in my muddy little pond. I cannot go South with you."

"Oh, yes you can," said the Gray Goose. "We will get a strong stick. I will take one end in my bill and Brother White Goose will take the other end in his bill. Then you will take the middle of the stick in your mouth and hold on tightly."

"That will be great fun," cried Little Green Turtle. "You are very kind, White Goose and Gray Goose. And I shall be very glad to go to the beautiful South with you."

"But there is one thing you must remember," said the White Goose. "You must not speak a single word while you are in the air."

"Yes," said the Gray Goose, "if you open your mouth, you will let go of the stick and fall to the ground. Not a single word. Can you remember that?"

"Oh, yes, indeed," answered Little Green Turtle, "I can remember that easily. I will not speak a single word on the whole journey."

So the geese flew off and came back with a stick. The White Goose took one end in his bill, and the Gray Goose took the other end in his bill. And Little Green Turtle took the middle of the stick in his mouth.

Off started the Gray Goose and the White Goose with Little Green Turtle holding the stick between them.

Up, up, up in the sky they flew, far above the plumey tops of the palm trees.

"What fun it is to go sailing through the air like this," thought Little Green Turtle.

When they passed over the village where the little children lived, the geese flew lower. Little Green Turtle could see his young friends who came to play in his muddy pond. They saw him, too, and they called out to one another:

"There is Little Green Turtle up in the sky. I wonder where he is going with the two geese!"

"I am going on a wonderful journey to the South to see a pool that is as blue as the sky and as clear as glass," he wanted to call down, but he remembered just in time that he must not speak, so he kept his mouth shut tight.

"What a silly way to travel!" the children cried, "holding on to a stick like that." And they laughed and pointed their fingers.

"It is not at all a silly way to travel. It is a very good way," Little Green Turtle wanted to call down, but he remembered in time that he must not speak a word, and so he kept his mouth shut tight.

"Little Green Turtle is always talking," cried the children. "He will never be able to keep from talking on a long journey."

That was more than Little Green Turtle could stand.

"I can, too," he cried. "I am not going to speak a word on the whole journey."

But alas, Little Green Turtle had opened his mouth to say this and he lost his hold on the stick. Down, down he fell, down to the feet of the little children.

"Poor Little Green Turtle," said one of them picking him up kindly. "He could not stop talking!"

SNOW-WHITE AND ROSE-RED

THERE once was a poor widow who lived in a lonely little cottage with a garden in front, where two rose-trees bloomed, one of which bore a white rose and the other a red. The widow had two children, who were like the rose-trees, for one was called Snow-white and the other Rose-red.

The two children loved each other so dearly that whenever they went out together they walked hand in hand. Very often they went out into the woods by themselves to pick berries, and the wild beasts would not harm them.

The children lived a very happy life with their dear mother in their pretty cottage home. In the evenings the mother would say, "Snow-white, bolt the door," and then they seated themselves round the hearth, and the mother put on her spectacles and read to them out of a favorite book, while the girls sat at their spinning wheels and listened.

One winter's evening, as they all sat comfortably together, someone knocked at the door as though he wished to be let in.

"Quick, Rose-red," said the mother, "open the door. Very likely some poor wanderer has come to seek shelter."

Rose-red ran to pull back the bolt and open the door, thinking to see a poor man, but instead, a great black bear pushed his head in and looked at them.

Rose-red screamed with fright, and Snow-white ran to hide herself behind her mother's bed.

But the bear told them not to be afraid, for he would not hurt them. "Please let me in. I am half frozen with the cold," he said, "and only wish to warm myself a little."

"Poor fellow," answered the mother; "lie down by the fire, but see that you do not burn your thick fur coat."

Then she called the children and told them to have no fear, for the bear would not harm them but was honest and respectable.

So Snow-white and Rose-red crept out from their hiding-places and were not the least afraid of the bear, who asked the children to brush the snow from his fur for him. They fetched a broom and brushed the thick black coat till not a single flake remained, and then the bear stretched himself comfortably in front of the fire and growled gently with content.

Before long the children were quite at home with their clumsy guest, playing all sorts of tricks upon him. The bear seemed well pleased with this treatment, though, and when they became a little too rough, he would cry comically, "Please, children, don't kill me."

When bedtime came the mother told the bear that he might spend the night beside the hearth, and so be sheltered from the cold and storm.

As soon as morning dawned, the two children opened the door, and he trotted away across the snow and was lost to sight in the wood. But from that day on, the bear came to them every night at the same time, laid himself down beside the hearth, and let the children play pranks with him as they liked, and they soon grew so accustomed to him that they never thought of bolting the door until their friend had arrived.

When the spring came and the whole world was fresh and green, the bear told Snow-white one morning that he would not be able to visit them again all through the summer months.

"Where are you going, dear bear?" asked Snow-white.

"I must stay in the woods and guard my treasures from the wicked dwarfs. In the winter, when the ground is frozen hard, they cannot work their way through it and are obliged to stay below in their caves; but now that the warm sun has thawed the earth, they will soon break upward and come to steal what they can find, and that which once goes into their caves seldom comes out again."

Snow-white grieved sadly over the parting. As she unbolted the door and the bear hurried through, a piece of his coat caught on the latch and was torn off, and it seemed to the child that she saw a glimmer of gold beneath it, but she was not sure. The bear ran quickly away, and soon disappeared behind the trees.

Some time afterwards the mother sent the children into the woods to gather sticks. They came to a great tree that lay felled on the ground. Beside it something very strange-looking kept jumping up and down in the grass.

At first they could not make out what it was, but as they came nearer they saw that it was a dwarf, with an old withered face and a long snow-white beard. The end of his beard had been caught fast in a split in the tree, and the creature jumped about like a little dog at the end of a string and knew not how to help himself.

He glared at the little girls with his fiery red eyes and screamed, "Why do you stand staring there instead of coming to help me?"

"What have you been doing, little man?" asked Rose-red.

"You silly, prying goose," answered the dwarf; "if you *must* know, I was splitting the tree to get some small pieces of wood for the kitchen. The large logs that you use would burn up our food in no time. We don't need to cook such a quantity as you great greedy folk. I had just driven the wedge firmly in and everything seemed right enough when it slipped on the smooth wood and popped out, so that the tree closed up in a second, catching my beautiful white beard as it did so; and now I cannot get it out again, and you foolish milk-faced creatures stand and laugh at me. Oh, how horrid you are!"

The children tried with all their might to help the old man, but they could not loosen his beard, and so Rose-red said she would run and fetch someone to help them.

"You stupid thing!" snarled the dwarf. "Why go and fetch others when you are two too many already? Can't you think of something better than that?"

"Have patience," said Snow-white. "I know what to do." And drawing her scissors from her pocket, she cut off the end of the old man's beard.

As soon as the dwarf was free he grabbed a bag of gold that was hidden among the roots of the tree, threw it across his shoulders, and grumbled out, "What clumsy folk, to be sure—to cut off a piece of my beautiful beard! Bad luck to you!" and then, without so much as a word of thanks to the children, away he went.

Some time afterwards Snow-white and Rose-red went to catch fish for dinner, and as they neared the brook, they saw something that looked like a grasshopper hopping along towards the water. They ran to it and soon recognized the dwarf.

"What *are* you doing?" said Rose-red; "surely you don't want to jump into the water?"

"I'm not quite such an idiot as that," shrieked the dwarf. "Can't you see that the horrid fish is pulling me in?"

The little man had been sitting fishing when the wind entangled his beard with the fishing-line. Just at that moment a large fish took the bait and the little weak creature was not strong enough to pull it out.

So the fish had the upper hand and was drawing the dwarf towards it. It is true the dwarf clutched at the grass and rushes as he went along, but it was all in vain, and he was forced to follow every movement of the fish, so that he was in great danger of being dragged into the water.

The children came just at the right moment. They held the little man fast and tried to disentangle the line, but they could not do so, and at last there was nothing to do but to bring out the scissors and snip off a little piece of his beard.

The dwarf was very angry when he saw what they had done.

"Is it good manners," he yelled, "to spoil a person's face like that, you toads? Not content with having shortened my beard, you must cut the best part out of it. May you go barefoot all your days!"

Then he seized a bag of pearls that lay hidden in the reeds, marched off without another word, and disappeared behind a stone.

It happened that soon afterwards the mother sent her two little girls into town to buy needles and thread, and laces and ribbons. On their way home they again met the dwarf. He had emptied his sack of precious stones upon a smooth place, little thinking to be surprised by anyone at such a late hour. The evening sun shone upon the glistening heap of gems and made them sparkle and flash so prettily that the children stood still to look at them.

"Why do you stand gaping there?" screamed the dwarf, his ashen grey face crimson with wrath. He would have continued to scold but at that moment loud growls were heard, and a big black bear came shambling out of the wood.

In terror the dwarf sprang towards his cave, but the bear was too near, and he could not reach it. Then he cried in his despair, "Dear Mr. Bear, spare me, I pray you, and I will give you all my treasures. Look at these precious stones; they shall all be yours if only you will spare my life. I am such a little fellow you would scarcely feel me between your teeth, but here are these two wicked girls—take them and eat them; you will find them tender morsels, and as fat as young quails."

The bear took no heed of his words, but gave the wicked creature one stroke with his paw, and he never moved again.

The two little girls had begun to run away, but the bear now called to them, "Snow-white, Rose-red, do not be afraid. If you will wait for me, I will come with you."

They recognized his voice at once and stood still, and as the bear came up to them, his fur coat suddenly fell from him, and he stood there, a handsome young man, dressed all in shining gold.

"I am a King's son," he said, "and I was condemned by the wicked dwarf, who had stolen all my treasures, to become a bear and run wild in the woods until I should be released by his death. He has now received his well-earned reward."

When they grew up, the Prince married little Snow-white while Rose-red was betrothed to his brother, and they divided between them all the beautiful treasures that the dwarf had collected in his cave.

The poor old mother went to live with her dear children, and took with her the two rose-trees from her little garden. These she planted close to her window, and every year they were covered with the most beautiful red and white roses that ever were seen.

PUSS-IN-BOOTS

By Reginald Wright Kauffman

Long years ago, a miller's will
    Distinctly stated that
He left to his three sons his mill,
    His donkey and his cat.

The oldest son received the mill,
    Which he had learned to run;
The donkey then the miller left
    To his next oldest son.

"Oh, no!" the youngest son complained,
    "I don't think much of that:
There's nothing left for me at all
    Except a useless cat!"

Then something touched him on the hand;
    He heard a gentle purr
And, looking down, he saw the cat
    And stroked its glossy fur.

"Meow!" said Puss; "and please be kind—
    Do what you can afford.
For kindness to an animal
    Is sure to bring reward.

"Buy me a pair of hunters' boots
    As high as is my knee,
For stones and prickles cut my feet—
    Then leave the rest to me."

Puss got his boots, and in the woods
    He spread a sack out wide;
He put some bran, which rabbits love,
    Deep in the sack's inside.

The rabbits came to get the bran;
    They sniffed about the sack;
Then crawled right in. Puss closed its top
    And flung it on his back.

The cat then hid his master's clothes;
    And when the King drove by,

That cat set up a caterwaul—
    You know how cats can cry.

Now, maybe twenty miles away,
    Beyond the rabbits' wood,
The palace of the country's King
    Beside a river stood.

So Puss, when he'd some rabbits rare,
    Did a surprising thing:
He took the best and trotted off
    To call upon the King!

"Get out!" the servants cried—said Puss,
    "You've got to let me pass!
My master is a marquis born—
    The Lord of Carabas!"

"He had good hunting-luck today
    And ordered me to bring
The best of all his rabbits as
    A present to the King."

Of Carabas those serving-men
    Had never seen a trace—
And this was not surprising; for
    There wasn't such a place—

But still it sounded all so fine
    And grand and everything,
And so they let Puss take the gift
    And give it to the King.

Then each day Puss would call again
    With rabbits more and more,
Until the kindly king felt sure
    He'd heard that name before.

Now, all this time the youngest son,
    As you may well suppose,
Was very poor. Said Puss: "Come on;
    I'll get you proper clothes!"

Puss led him to the riverside
    And made him go to swim—
Puss knew the King drove by each day
    Before the light grew dim.

"Meow! Help, help! Meow!" he screamed;
    "My master drowns, alas!
O King, be kind, and help me save
    The Lord of Carabas!

"Thieves stripped him of his gems and clothes
    And in the water tossed
My Marquis. Hurry, hurry, please,
    Or he will soon be lost!"

The lad was saved. The King declared:
    "You'll be my palace-guest."
Then all in silk and velvet soft
    He had the young man dressed.

"I'll drive you home," the Monarch said
    Next day. "Oh," thought the Cat,
"My master's house is far too plain—
    I'll have to see to that!"

He ran ahead and told the folk:
    "When soon the King shall pass,
He orders you to cheer, 'Hurrah,
    Our Lord of Carabas!'

"His Majesty will much be pleased
    If this is what you do;
But if you don't, he says he'll make
    Mincemeat of all of you!"

The people did as they were told;
    The King was very glad
To think that all the fields he saw
    Were owned by this young lad.

Next Puss an Ogre's castle spied;
    The Ogre laughed to see
A Puss-in-Boots. "Come in," he said
    ("I'll eat you soon," thought he.)

"Sir Ogre, I am told," purred Puss,
    "That, if you want to, you
Can change yourself to something else—
    I don't believe it's true."

"You'll see!" the Ogre roared, and changed
    Into a lion; then:

"I'll eat you when I am myself!"—
    And was himself again.

Poor Puss was scared, but said: "You are
    So big yourself, you can
Of course change into anything
    That's bigger than a man;

"But not to something small—a rat
    Or mouse; that's hard, you see.
A bargain; if you fail in this,
    You'll kindly set me free!"

"Done!" said the Ogre—and became
    A mouse. —"My turn to sup!"
Cried Puss. He pounced upon the mouse
    And straightway ate it up!

Puss ran to meet the King and said:
    "Come in and have no fear;
This castle is my master's house:
    You're always welcome here!"

The lad stood up and told the truth:
    "Your Majesty, alas,
I'm nothing but a miller's son—
    No Lord of Carabas."

So, when the story all was told,
    A strange thing came to pass;
The King said: "Lad, I make you now
    True Lord of Carabas.

"This Puss-in-Boots has said some things
    Not quite true to the letter;
But cats are not like boys and girls
    And don't know any better—

"Because you're kind to animals,
    As I could plainly see,
Henceforth you are what Puss-in-Boots
    Has hoped that you might be.

"My Princess-daughter shall become
    Your loving wife."—And that
Is what the miller's son received
    For kindness to a cat.

CINDERELLA

Illustrated by Lois Lenski

ONCE upon a time there was a little girl who lived alone with her father. Her own kind mother was dead, and her father, who loved her very dearly, was afraid his beloved child was sometimes lonely. So he married a grand lady who had two daughters of her own, and who, he thought, would be kind and good to his little one. But no sooner did the stepmother enter her new home than she began to show her true character. Her stepdaughter was so much prettier and sweeter than her own children that she was jealous of her and gave her all the hard work to do, while the two proud sisters spent their time dressing finely and enjoying grand parties and entertainments.

The only pleasure the poor child had was to spend her evenings sitting in the chimney-corner, resting her weary limbs, and for this reason her sisters mockingly nicknamed her Cinderella. The sisters' fine clothes made Cinderella feel very shabby but, in her little torn frock and ragged shoes, she was a thousand times more lovely than they.

Now, it chanced that the King's son gave a grand ball to which he invited all the lords and ladies in the country, and amongst the rest, Cinderella and her two sisters were asked. For days the sisters talked of nothing but what they should wear and who they hoped to meet.

When at last the great day arrived, Cinderella was kept running about from early till late, decking the sisters and dressing their hair.

"Don't you wish you were going to the ball?" said one of them.

"Indeed I do," sighed the poor little maid. The sisters burst out laughing. "A pretty spectacle you would be," they said rudely. Then, stepping carefully into their carriage so that they might not crush their fine clothes, they drove away.

Cinderella went back to her chimney-corner and tried not to feel envious, but tears gathered in the pretty eyes and trickled down the sorrowful little face.

"Do not cry, child," said a silvery voice. "You, too, may go to the ball."

Cinderella started and raised her eyes. Who could it be? Then in a moment she knew— it was her fairy Godmother!

"Run quickly into the garden, and bring the largest pumpkin you can find."

In a few moments Cinderella was back with a splendid pumpkin. Her Godmother scooped out the inside, and with one touch of the wand, the pumpkin was a golden coach, lined with white satin.

"Now, child, quick—the mouse-trap from the pantry!"

"Here it is, Godmother," said Cinderella breathlessly. One by one six fat sleek mice passed through the trap-door. As each appeared, a touch of the wand transformed it into a cream-colored horse, fit for a queen.

"Now, Cinderella, can you find a coach-man?"

"There is a large gray rat in the rat-trap— would he do, Godmother?"

"Run and fetch him, child, and then I can judge." So Cinderella ran to fetch the rat, and her Godmother said he was just made for a coachman. Next, six lizards from behind the pumpkin-frame became six footmen in splendid liveries.

"Oh! Godmother," she cried, "it is all so lovely!" Then suddenly she thought of her shabby frock.

But just at that moment, her Godmother's wand tapped her lightly on the shoulder, and in the place of the shabby frock, there was a gleam of satin, silver, and pearls. The gown was white as snow, and as dazzling; round the hem hung a fringe of diamonds, and lace billowed about the throat and arms. Her feet shimmered in tiny glass slippers.

"Come," said the Godmother, "or you will be late. Enjoy yourself, my dear child. Only remember, if you stay at the palace one instant after midnight, your coach and servants will vanish, and you will be little Cinderella once more!"

A few moments later, the coach dashed into the royal courtyard, the door was flung open, and Cinderella alighted. As she walked slowly up the richly-carpeted staircase, there was a murmur of admiration, and the King's son hastened to meet her. "Never," said he to himself, "have I seen anyone so lovely!"

The evening passed away in a dream of delight, Cinderella dancing with no one but the handsome young Prince. The two sisters could not recognize their ragged little sister in the beautiful and graceful lady to whom the Prince paid so much attention.

But the hours flew by so happily and so swiftly that Cinderella forgot her promise, until she happened to look at a clock and saw that it was on the stroke of twelve. With a cry of alarm she fled from the room, dropping, in her haste, one of the little glass slippers. The Prince hurried after her, but when he reached the entrance hall, the beautiful Princess had vanished, and there was no one to be seen but a forlorn little beggar-maid creeping away.

Poor little Cinderella!—the fire was out when she reached home, and no Godmother was waiting to receive her; so she sat down in the chimney-corner to await her sisters' return. When they came in they could speak of nothing but the wonderful things that had happened at the ball. A beautiful Princess had been there, they said, but had disappeared just as the clock struck twelve, and though the Prince had searched everywhere for her, he had been unable to find her. "He was beside himself with grief," said the elder sister, "for there is no doubt he hoped to make her his bride."

Cinderella listened in silence to all they had to say, and slipping her hand into her pocket, felt that the one glass slipper was safe, for it was the only thing of all her grand apparel that remained to her.

On the following morning there was a great noise of trumpets and drums, and a procession passed through the town, at the head of which rode the King's son. Behind him came a herald bearing a velvet cushion, upon which rested a little glass slipper. The herald blew a blast upon the trumpet, and then read a proclamation saying that the King's son would wed any lady in the land who could fit the slipper upon her foot.

Of course, the sisters tried to squeeze their feet into the slipper, but it was of no use—they were much too large. Then Cinderella shyly begged that she might try. How the sisters laughed with scorn when the Prince knelt to fit the slipper on the cinder-maid's foot; but what was their surprise when it slipped on with the greatest ease, and the next moment Cinderella produced the other from her pocket! Once more she stood in the slippers, and once more the sisters saw before them the lovely Princess who was to be the Prince's bride. For at the touch of the magic shoes, the gray frock disappeared, and in place of it she wore the beautiful robe her Godmother had given her.

The Prince could not bear to part from her again, so he brought her back to the palace with him, and they were married that very day. In the place of honor sat the fairy Godmother. And in time they came to be King and Queen and lived happily ever after.

THE FROG PRINCE

Illustrated by Tasha Tudor

LONG ago, when wishes really came true, there lived a King and his beautiful daughter who was so lovely that the sun could not but marvel when it shone upon her face. Every day when the sun was in the sky, the Princess would sit on the cool stones of the palace well, tossing a golden ball high in the air, watching the sun make it shine and glisten to her delight. But one day she accidentally tossed her ball too high, and when it came down, she could not catch it. Instead, it fell deep into the well. The Princess cried bitterly.

"Tell me why you are crying, Princess," a voice said. The Princess looked toward the voice, and through her tears she saw the broad, ugly face of a frog.

"Oh, please, frog," said the Princess. "If you bring me back my ball, which has fallen into the well, anything in the world you wish for will be yours."

"I care nothing for wealth," said the frog. "Make me your favorite companion. Let me sit beside you at the table, eat from your plate, and drink from your cup. Let me sleep on your bed at night. If you promise, I will dive into the well and fetch your golden ball."

"What nonsense," thought the Princess, but agreed to grant his wish. The frog dived under the water and returned with her ball. Without so much as a word of thanks, the Princess picked up the ball and skipped home to the palace.

"Wait! Wait for me!" croaked the frog. But the Princess did not listen and quite forgot her promise to the frog.

The next evening, the Princess and the King were eating dinner when they heard a splashing and a plopping on the front steps. The Princess ran to the door. There, squatting on the doorstep, was the frog. She slammed the door and ran back to her place at the table, for she was very frightened.

"Whatever is the matter, my child?" asked the King. "Who is at the door?"

"No one, Father, but a hideous frog."

"And what does such a creature want with you?"

"I promised the frog that if he fetched my ball from the well, I would be his friend. But, oh, Father, I never dreamed he would leave the well."

"A promise is a promise," said the King sternly. "Now go and let in your playmate."

With great reluctance, the Princess opened the door. The frog followed her to her chair. "Lift me up beside you," he croaked. She shuddered but remembered her promise and placed him on the chair beside her. Then he asked to be set on the table, where he might reach her plate and cup. And when it was time for bed, he asked to sleep on the pillow by her head. There, to the Princess's disgust, he stayed until dawn.

The next morning, the frog slid off her pillow and onto the floor. But as soon as his feet touched the floor, he was no longer a frog. He had become a handsome Prince.

"You see," he said to the Princess, "a wicked magician cast a spell on me. The curse could only be broken when I became your friend." Then, he really did become her favorite companion. And when they grew up, they married and lived happily ever after.

102

THE SHOEMAKER AND THE ELVES

Illustrated by Lucille W. and H. C. Holling

ONCE upon a time there was a kind, honest man who worked hard all day long making shoes. His good wife bustled around cooking the meals and keeping their little house tidy and clean.

One day the shoemaker had not a single penny left. The soup kettle was empty, and the fire had gone out, for there were no more sticks to keep it burning.

All that the good shoemaker had left was enough leather to make one pair of shoes. But he did not begin to whine and complain. No, instead he set to work and cut leather just the right shape to make a pair of shoes. Then he laid it out on his workbench and went whistling off to bed.

"Tomorrow morning," he said to himself, "I will get up early and make the shoes. Somebody will be sure to buy them."

When the good shoemaker went into the shop the next morning, there on the bench lay the finest pair of shoes he had ever seen. They were made of the leather he had cut out the day before and were sewed with the tiniest stitches imaginable. Astonished and delighted, he called his good wife, and she was as much pleased and surprised as he.

That day a man came into the shop and saw the fine pair of shoes. He bought them at once and gave the shoemaker enough money to buy leather for two pairs of shoes.

In the evening, the good shoemaker cut out the new leather and laid it out on the workbench.

"I will get up bright and early in the morning and make the shoes," he said to himself cheerfully as he went whistling off to bed.

In the morning, there on the bench lay two fine pairs of shoes all neatly and beautifully stitched from the leather the shoemaker had cut out the night before.

That day two men came into the shop and each bought a pair of the fine shoes. They paid the shoemaker so well that he had money to buy leather for four pairs of shoes.

He set to work at once and cut out the leather for four pairs of shoes. That night he laid it on the workbench, climbed into bed, and fell asleep at once. In the morning, there upon the workbench lay four pairs of shoes all neatly and beautifully stitched.

These fine shoes brought him in enough money to buy more leather and plenty of good things to put in the soup kettle, as well as wood to keep the fire burning.

Every night the good shoemaker laid out the work on the bench, and in the morning, no matter how much he had left, the leather was made into shoes.

The good shoemaker and his wife were now very comfortable and happy, but they wondered very much who had been doing so much work for them.

"Let us leave a light burning tonight," said the shoemaker. "Then we will hide in the corner of the workshop and see who it is who has brought us all this good luck."

So the good shoemaker and his wife left a light burning and hid themselves behind a curtain in the corner of the shop.

They waited for a long time and nothing happened. Then just as the clock struck twelve, two tiny elves came dancing in at the door and jumped upon the bench.

They wore no clothes at all, but they carried with them tiny hammers, scissors, thimbles and needles—all the very smallest that the shoemaker had ever seen. They picked up the pieces of leather and began to put them together.

Tap, tap, tap. Pound, pound, pound. Stitch, stitch, stitch. How the tiny fingers flew! The shoemaker and his wife had never seen shoes made so quickly. And every stitch was perfect, and every nail exactly in the right place.

Before long all the leather the shoemaker had cut out the night before had been turned into shoes. Then the two little elves began to skip merrily around, and just as the clock struck two they danced out of the window.

As you can imagine, the good shoemaker and his wife were very much surprised to find out how the shoes had been made.

"I wish there was some way we could thank these kind little people who have brought us so much good luck," said the shoemaker.

"They looked so cold with nothing to cover them," said the shoemaker's wife. "I have a mind to make them each a little suit of clothes to keep them warm."

"And I will make them each a tiny pair of shoes for their bare, cold little feet," the shoemaker added.

So they both set to work. The good wife cut out two little coats of fine green cloth, two little waistcoats of yellow, two little pairs of trousers of blue, and two little caps of red. She sewed them with the finest of stitches. And the good shoemaker cut out two tiny pairs of shoes with long pointed toes and hammered them with his smallest nails.

When the night came the good shoemaker laid the two tiny pairs of pointed shoes on the bench and his good wife laid the two tiny suits of clothes beside them. Then they left a light burning and hid behind the curtain in the workshop.

Just as the clock struck twelve, the two tiny elves came dancing in the door. When they saw the two little suits of clothes and the two little pairs of shoes, they clapped their hands, laughed aloud, and put them on as quickly as possible.

The little blue trousers, the little yellow waistcoats, the little green coats, the little red caps, and the little pointed shoes fitted perfectly. The elves smoothed their new coats with their hands, buttoned their yellow waistcoats, and smiled happily at each other. Then they began to dance, and when the clock struck two they danced away out of the window.

The shoemaker and his wife never saw them again, but the elves must have sent them good luck, for ever after that, the good couple had all they needed.

THE UGLY DUCKLING

Illustrated by George and Doris Hauman

MOTHER Duck once built her nest beside the wall of a great castle. There was a moat around the wall that was filled with water in which many ducks and geese swam.

Mother Duck found it very lonesome sitting on her eggs, day after day, and she did not have many visitors. Her friends liked better to swim about in the moat than to sit and keep her company.

However, she knew that she must not let her eggs grow cold, so she sat on them patiently, day after day. One morning she heard a crack, and a tiny yellow duck pushed its way out of the egg. Soon there was another crack—and another—and another—until every egg except one had broken. This last egg was much larger than the others.

As Mother Duck sat wondering why it did not crack, old Grandmother Duck, who was swimming by, waddled ashore.

"How are you?" she quacked.

"Very well, thank you" Mother Duck replied. "All my eggs have hatched except one. Come in and see my pretty ducklings."

"What fine ducklings," the old Grandmother said. "But why waste time sitting on that large egg any longer? I'm sure it's a turkey's egg, and a little turkey is a great bother to a duck. I know because I hatched one long ago. He was so afraid of the water that he wouldn't even wet his toes."

"I may as well sit on it a little longer," said Mother Duck, "I've sat so long now, that I'd like to finish the hatching."

"Do as you like," said the old Grandmother Duck, waddling back to the moat. "But remember that I warned you!"

The next day the large egg cracked and out came the strangest looking creature ever to come out of an egg. Instead of being yellow and fluffy, like the other ducklings, it was an ugly greenish-gray color, and it had a long neck and long awkward legs.

"He's the ugliest child I ever had," thought Mother Duck. But she treated him kindly and tried not to let him feel that he was different from the others.

Soon she decided that it was time to teach her little ones to swim. She led the way from the nest and waddled ahead of them to the moat.

"Quack! Quack!" she called. "Follow me into the water and use your feet as I use mine."

The ducklings waddled into the water and spread their little webbed feet. In a few minutes they were swimming as well as Mother Duck herself.

"My Ugly Duckling swims as well as the others, so Grandmother Duck was wrong when she said he would be a turkey. But he certainly is ugly, poor child," thought Mother Duck.

"Now we're going to the poultry yard," she called. She led the way out of the water, and the little ones followed. A few minutes later they waddled into the poultry yard, where there were many other ducks, as well as geese and hens and turkeys. Such a quacking and clucking and gobbling you never heard!

Everyone stared at the Ugly Duckling, and a young drake laughed out loud.

"Did anyone ever see such a ridiculous-looking bird?" he said. With his sharp bill he pecked at the poor little Ugly Duckling.

"Stop!" said Mother Duck. "I will not have my duckling ill-treated." Then, the largest, most scornful turkey in the yard came up and looked at the frightened little bird.

"Gobble! Gobble! Gobble!" he said, "Who ever brought this ugly duckling into our poultry yard?"

"Keep away," Mother Duck said. "I will not allow anyone to torment him."

But Mother Duck could not be beside the Ugly Duckling all the time, and whenever she was away from him for a moment, someone teased him or pecked at him. The Ugly Duckling was given no peace. Even his own brothers and sisters made fun of him, and the girl who came out to feed them kicked him away.

Day after day things grew worse. The Ugly Duckling was treated so badly that he decided to run away. He ran toward the fence, spreading his wings, and by using all his strength he managed to fly over it. The little birds in the bushes where he landed flew away in fright. "This is because I am so ugly that I terrify them," he thought sadly.

He traveled on until he reached a great marsh where crowds of wild ducks were swimming. The Ugly Duckling swam out among them, bowing politely this way and that, as Mother Duck had taught him to do. The wild ducks made fun of him, but they did not peck him as the birds in the poultry yard had done.

"You're very ugly," one of them told him, "we don't mind having you around but don't try to marry into any of our families."

The poor little duck had no thought of marriage. All he wanted was a chance to find food and a comfortable place to sleep. He swam around the marsh and found plenty to eat and spent the night under some tall rushes at the edge of the water.

Before long the wild ducks spread their wings and flew away. The Ugly Duckling was left alone in the marsh. The days grew colder, and food was harder and harder to find. At length the water began to freeze and the place where he swam became smaller and smaller. One morning he was frozen in and could not move. He thought the end of his life had come, but a peasant who was passing broke the ice with his wooden shoe and carried the half frozen little duck home. Here he soon thawed out in the heat of the cottage.

The peasant had two children who wanted to play with the little bird, but the Ugly Duckling was afraid of them and flew wildly about. He flopped into the milk pan, and when the peasant's wife shouted at him he flew from the milk into the butter crock and then into the

flour barrel. By this time he was no longer gray but white with flour. The poor woman ran at him with the fire tongs, but fortunately the door was open and the Ugly Duckling managed to escape.

The rest of the winter was a time of great suffering for him. He almost starved, and the only shelter he could find was a clump of dried rushes. But he lived through the cold months, and when the spring came, the sun began to warm the marsh, and the plants began to grow. Soon the Ugly Duckling felt warm and comfortable. Ugly as he was, he felt the hope of Spring.

The song birds that had flown south for the winter began to come back. As the Ugly Duckling heard their songs, he felt a desire to fly. He spread his wings and rose from the ground. His wings had grown long and strong, and they made a rushing sound as he flew into the air.

How beautiful the world looked! Apple trees were in bloom and little streams rippled through green fields. The Ugly Duckling flew on and on, enjoying the warm sun and the blue sky and the lovely places over which he passed. After a while he saw a great house with a beautiful garden. In the garden was a pond that looked like a sheet of clear glass.

The Ugly Duckling swooped down and lighted on the pond. "How I should love to live here," he thought. Just then he saw three wonderful birds come out of the bushes and walk down to the water. They had gleaming white plumage and long graceful necks.

"They must be swans, the royal birds," the Ugly Duckling thought. He felt sad as he looked at them. "This pond must belong to them, and they will not allow me to stay," he thought. He was about to spread his wings and fly away but a great sadness came over him.

As the three swans swam toward him, he bowed his head. But as he looked at his reflection in the clear water, he saw that he was no longer gray and ugly. His neck was long and graceful and his plumage was glistening white, like that of the three swans. When they came close to him they did not peck at him or make fun of him. They stroked him gently with their bills and welcomed him to the pond.

Just then two children ran out of the house, bringing bread for the swans.

"There's a new one," called the little boy.

"Yes, and how beautiful it is," the little girl replied, "more beautiful than any of the others."

When they heard the words, the three swans bowed their graceful necks in honor of their new comrade.

How happy he was! To be welcomed by the most beautiful birds in the world! He shook his white plumes, stretched his powerful wings, and said joyfully: "It does not matter that one was hatched in a duck's nest, if one came from a swan's egg. I never dreamed that such happiness was in store for me, in the days when I was called the Ugly Duckling."

THE END